Time

Time

Jesus in Relationships
A Novel

Alan Sorem

RESOURCE *Publications* · Eugene, Oregon

TIME
Jesus in Relationships: A Novel

Resource Publications
An Imprint of Wipf and Stock Publishers
199 W. 8th Ave., Suite 3
Eugene, OR 97401
www.wipfandstock.com

ISBN 13: 978-1-55635-962-0
Manufactured in the U.S.A.

For my grandchildren,
Leo and Sigrid
Fides et Fortis

Names

Hebrew	English
Yeshua	Jesus
Yosef	Joseph
Miriam	Mary
Elisheva	Elizabeth
Yohannon	John
Rebekah	Rebecca
Yaakob	Jacob/James
Yosa	Little Joseph
Yehudah	Judah
Shimeon	Simon
Zebadya	Zebedee
Philippos (Greek)	Philip
Andreas (Greek)	Andrew

Places

Yerushalayim	Jerusalem
Nehar ha Yarden	River Jordan
Kapharnaum	Capernaum

CHAPTER 1

TWO ABREAST, SHOULDER TO shoulder, the line of men shuffled forward. Not prisoners but rather a line of hopeful humanity pressing forward to the riverbank and the waters just beyond. The men were silent, each individual filled with an anticipation common to all of them: rich man, poor man preparing for the cleansing ritual of baptism that would bring liberation to a new life of commitment to the Lord.

The day had begun sunny but now the clouds overhead were darkening. A light breeze swirled the desert sand over by the grove of trees where all the tents for pilgrims were pitched. Yeshua could see women walking among the trees, waiting for their turn to form a line once the men finished. A child's sudden cry came, followed by the soft voice of a mother. The cry subsided.

As he slowly moved onward in the line together with the man on his right, Yeshua thought of the events that had brought him to this day. The episode in the Temple that occurred when he was twelve. His study of scripture until it was imprinted on his brain. The recent visit of his kinsman, son of Zechariah. Most important, the sudden death of his father, Yosef, that prompted his mother to tell him details about his birth.

Nearing the river, an older man regulated the line. "Single file, now. Single file," he chanted as he eyed the clouds overhead. The line thinned and reformed to single file. Some men complained. They wanted to get to the river quickly to be cleansed of their sins.

To his right there was another line of men, coming from the river. Their tunics were drenched but their faces glowed with a radiant joy. Most held up their hands in prayer. Others softly sang a praise psalm of the Temple. Yeshua wished Yosef had lived to see this day.

He continued to move slowly forward. At last the man ahead of him reached the river. A boy in shepherd's clothes was clambering up the side of the bank. From his shaggy hair rivulets of water dripped, further wetting his soaked rough clothing. He was smiling broadly at the men in the line moving forward. "What a glorious day," he shouted. "Praise the Lord." A young man wearing a much-mended white cloak held up a hand for the line to wait. In the river an elderly man dressed in the cloak of a Temple priest was raised from the river water. The young man in the white cloak nodded and the person in front of Yeshua carefully stepped on stones that formed a path down to the river and waded toward the three men who were baptizing. One of the three was Yeshua's kinsman Yohannon. For just a moment Yeshua thought again of Yosef, but he smiled as he realized Yosef was there with him in spirit.

And then it was his turn. His Time.

CHAPTER 2

Two MONTHS EARLIER IT had not been an easy death for his father.

Yosef had purchased a cartload of quality cedar wood in Selame at an excellent price. As he and his pony made their way south to Nazareth, the bright sunshine gave way to a gathering storm. Yosef urged the pony onwards, but they could not outrace the steady cold rain that soon fell.

Finding no shelter nearby, Yosef struggled onward with his valuable purchase. He and the pony at last reached home. Both were soaked and chilled to the bone. The pony was taken to the stable at the side of the house and rubbed down. But warm towels did not calm Yosef. His chest rumbling with a deep cough, he took to his bed and did not rise from it.

Through day and night his wife and seven children took turns keeping vigil at his bedside. Now, on the eighth day, the oldest son, Yeshua, watched over his father in the early hours before dawn. Miriam had wanted to stay but he quietly urged her to go his sisters' room. She went. He slipped into the chair his mother vacated.

"Call me if there's a change," Miriam whispered. He nodded and turned to Yosef. The raw gasping for breath had begun two days ago. Tonight the mixture in the tea had helped Yosef to sleep but the gasping was increasingly labored. His once-muscular frame was drawn in and shrunken.

Yeshua shifted in the chair for a more comfortable position. Years ago Yosef had made the chair and all the other furniture in the room: two chests for clothing, a simple bed frame, and a small table on which the single oil lamp illuminated the room. "He has a gift with wood," Miriam had often remarked.

The gasping changed, modulating to a quieter, less desperate sound. Yeshua wondered if it was a positive or negative sign.

The only other family member he had watched in death throes was his uncle. Cleopas was chasing a maverick ram when he fell in the field against a sharp rock that sliced through his cloak and cut his chest open. The shepherd ran to the village. Yeshua and others had hurried back to the field and carried Cleopas to his home. He, too, had had rasping breath before he died, just after sundown.

The breathing changed. Yeshua leaned closer and saw the twitching eyelids. His father was dreaming again. The mixture in the tea had not been strong enough to release him from his dreams.

Yosef's body jerked suddenly and his eyes opened, focused on his oldest son.

"Help me up." Effort at speaking cast spittle on his beard.

"Father, you must calm yourself.

"Help me up!"

The chair creaked as the son leaned forward and slid an arm under Yosef's shoulders and tilted upward. His father's eyes filled with tears.

"My beloved son." He paused for a moment, gathering more breath to speak. "Tell me again. The wonderful words of the prophet Micah."

Yeshua nodded. "'What does the Lord require of you? To do justice, and to love kindness, and to walk humbly in the way of the Lord.'"

Yosef stretched out a trembling hand and laid it on his son's head. "I give you my blessing." His hand fell back to his side. Yosef's eyes closed.

"Help your mother," he said weakly. "She has been a good wife."

The curtain at the doorway rustled as Miriam rushed in. Behind her, his two sisters peered into the room.

"I heard voices."

"He is struggling to speak," Yeshua replied. "I fear he is near the end."

Miriam knelt by the bed and began kissing her husband. "Yosef, oh my dear Yosef!"

His eyes opened. "Miriam," he said and cleared his throat. "Miriam." He paused for breath. "I was never the one to speak of it." He glanced towards Yeshua. "You must tell him."

Yosef's hands clutched at her as he tried to pull himself further up. His eyes implored her. "It is your story." He fell back. "Your story."

At the doorway, sisters Elisheva and Rebekah held the curtain to one side as their brothers poured into the small room. Yaakob, the next oldest to Yeshua, was the most alert, his eyes focused on his father. The face of Yosa, "Little Yosef," was grim. Yehuda rubbed sleep from his eyes as Shimeon, the youngest, limped into the room, his eyes moist with tears.

Yosef's gaze rested on the faces of his children and he mustered strength to speak.

"I love you all. You have been a blessing to me." He coughed harshly. "Listen to Yeshua."

The voice faded. Yosef gasped twice more. The eyes that had shone in the light of the lamp turned dim and cold.

Yeshua lowered him to the bed.

"He trusted me," Miriam said softly. "May the Lord bless him forever."

Yeshua glanced at her, puzzled by her words. She turned to him.

"Say the prayer," she murmured fiercely. "Say it now, while he is still warm."

There was no puzzle about these words. Yeshua nodded. He lifted his hands upward and spoke.

"Heavenly Father, our help in every time of trouble. May your great name be exalted and sanctified in the world, which you created according to your will. Establish your kingdom; may your salvation blossom and your anointed be near. Receive now your servant Yosef. May he hear your words of welcome, 'Come, O blessed faithful. Enter the joy of my heavenly home and rest from your labors.'" Yeshua paused. "So be it, now and forevermore."

Miriam and the others said in unison, "Dominion and fear are with him; he makes peace in his highest heaven."

Yeshua's hands lowered.

"Thank you," Miriam whispered. His sisters began the keening ululations of mourning. Beneath the sounds of grieving, she turned to Yeshua and spoke, her voice heavy with emotion.

"You are the head of our house now."

"Yes. But what is it you must tell me?"

"Not now. Once all has been done according to our ways." Miriam raised a hand to caress his face. "Yeshua," she whispered. Then she turned and fell across her husband's lifeless body, her cries mingling with those of her daughters and her tears falling alongside theirs.

Chapter 3

THE LONG NIGHT WAS over. At dawn Yeshua and two of the older leaders of the synagogue took Yosef's body in a plain cloth shroud to the burial cave in the hillside near the cemetery. Elisheva and Rebekah followed at a respectful distance behind them. Elisheva carried the sponges and water basin for washing the body, Rebekah, the spices for anointing and the white linen winding cloth.

The three men grunted as they pushed the large rolling stone away from the entrance to the cave. The cave had been hollowed out of the hillside by Yeshua's great-grandfather. There were a dozen other caves nestled at the foot of the hill; they were made by prosperous members of the synagogue to remedy overcrowding in the town cemetery.

Yeshua and one of the others carefully carried Yosef into the tomb and lowered him onto a stone slab laid atop stone plinths in the tomb's anteroom. Slowly they unwrapped the plain cloth to reveal the corpse. Returning to the small doorway, Yeshua beckoned to his sisters. He took the sponges and water basin and handed them inside the tomb. Then he took the other elements himself and returned to the anteroom.

The three men recited the burial prayers as they washed the body and dried it. The anointing spices were applied and then the winding cloth carefully was wrapped as Yeshua recited the final prayer.

They stood silent at the prayer's end. Yeshua looked to the side of the anteroom where a large chest stood. It had been made by his great-grandfather and contained his bones and those of his family members, as well as the bones of his grandfather's family.

And soon, the bones of my father will rest in that chest and later the bones of all my family, and myself as well, he thought. A sudden coolness came over him like a cloud shading the sun.

He nodded to the others. They lifted feet and head of the enshrouded figure and slowly moved to the inner room of the cave. It was a small space dominated by an earthen shelf to one side. The body was laid there.

After another moment of silence the two older men left the tomb, carrying the basin and sponges, which they handed on to the sisters. Yeshua carried the plain cloth and his father's nightshirt into the morning air.

Once the large stone was moved into position, Yeshua stood looking at it for a moment longer. *In three years I will come and remove the bones from the cloth and add them to the chest.*

He turned and joined the other four in the walk to the village.

In the afternoon they and many others dressed in their best clothes returned with the elderly rabbi of their synagogue.

After the customary prayers, the rabbi gave thanksgiving for the life of Yosef. Not only was Yosef a man of honor and peace, he said, but also he was a man well versed in the Law and the Prophets. The rabbi nodded approvingly at Yeshua, stating that Yosef's son took after his father and was known in the town for his own learning. Ah, remember the Passover when we thought young Yeshua was lost and all the time he was safely conversing with the elders of the Temple. What a joy that was! Then the rabbi reminded his listeners that thanks to the providential working of the Lord the people of the Nazareth congregation were not like followers of the Sadducees, who believed this life was all there is. No, Nazareth and other towns of Galilea followed the true and holy teachings of the Pharisees, who teach that the just and pure in heart know that their Redeemer lives and they will live in glory with the Holy One.

Yeshua waited for the words to end. He smiled as he thought of the feast that had been prepared for friends in the village and others who had come from afar to honor his father's life of craftsmanship and wisdom. It was almost time for the final prayers. The rabbi was an honored guest at the feast and understood that the meal would soon grow cold.

Yeshua looked around at the people standing with him in a semicircle around the tombstone.

Two men of the synagogue glanced at him. Their grown sons stood beside them.

Yeshua had a sudden recollection of how fierce Yosef had been with them so many years ago. Their sons had been taunting Shimeon as he limped homeward one day. Shimeon and the two sons—all three must have been no more than six years in age at the time.

"Born of imperfection," they had cried, fingers pointing as other children came from side streets to see what the fuss was about. "Child of sin!" Other words followed.

Shimeon had limped faster toward the door of the woodworking shop, where Yosef, Yeshua and Yaakob peered out at the commotion.

Yosef's face had turned dark red, and he yanked Shimeon into the shop and turned on his tormentors and the children who had gathered behind them.

"Go home, you idiots!" he had shouted, pointing at the two who were taunting. "I will come to see your fathers!"

Later he did and he took along the rabbi, a younger man then, as witness.

The story was all over the village by the evening. How Yosef and the rabbi had gone to meet the two fathers whose children had taunted Shimeon. No pleasantries were exchanged.

"Do you not remember my grandfather?" Yosef had said in a voice that could be heard in the street. The two fathers had nodded. "Do you not remember my father?" They had nodded again. "And do you know me?" Oh, yes, of course, they answered.

"Let us speak clearly to each other. What sin did my grandfather or father commit—what sin have I committed—that can be said to have been visited upon my poor lame child?"

"Yosef, Yosef , "one of the fathers replied, "the games of children. What was said is unseemly but not to be taken seriously. Mere words!"

"Words spoken with malice can pierce the heart deeper than the sharpest knife," Yosef retorted. "Shall our sons grow to manhood in this way?"

They were silent, casting glances at each other. Yosef continued, "Yes, my youngest son has a lame leg since birth. How this has come upon him as his lot I do not know. But I wish him to grow and live in the spirit of the words of the blessed Isaiah, 'Surely the Lord is my salvation. Therefore I will trust, and will not be afraid, for the Lord is my strength and my might.'"

Yosef had turned to the rabbi. "Rabbi, you are my witness. Do you know or have you heard of any sin I have committed to cause the Lord to visit affliction upon my son?"

"No. None."

Yosef turned back to the two fathers.

"The matter is settled. Let there be no more false accusations against my boy. Do we understand one another?"

Nods all around.

There were no more taunts in the days that followed, but as the rabbi and Yosef walked in the street, the rabbi spoke words that Yosef later repeated several times to Shimeon's four brothers.

"Take care, my friend. They are proud men and will remember this day for years to come."

On the occasions when he repeated the rabbi's words to Yeshua, Yaakob, Yosa and Yehudah, he gave each a long glance and said, "Look after your brother."

CHAPTER 4

TWO WEEKS PASSED. YESHUA and Yaakob were in the woodworking room. Yosa had taken the laden pony cart to make deliveries in the nearby villages.

The house was a large one for Nazareth. There were eight rooms spread about in a single storey, which included the workshop, plus a stable at the left side to shelter the donkey and milk cow and pony.

The house and the long garden behind testified to Yosef's prosperity. The house had one interesting feature: the workshop at the right side was the only room to have a wooden door, rather than a curtain, facing the central hallway. Yosef had crafted the door in earlier years to keep the younger children from bursting in with their games and disturbing his concentration as he turned the wood.

Years ago the two older brothers had moved from apprenticeship to status as partners with their father. Recently Yosa had joined them. Today Yosa was delivering furniture while the two older brothers completed the decorative finishing touches on several items of furniture ordered by a man in Kapharnaum. And soon they were to receive word from a friend in Caesarea Maritima concerning possible orders. The seaport, one of Herod the Great's massive projects, was now the headquarters of Pontius Pilate, the Roman prefect for central Palestine.

As he worked Yeshua thought once again about what his dying father had said to his mother. From his youth, Miriam and Yosef always had been open with him, in discipline and in instruction. What else could there be to say? When would she tell him? Perhaps it was an apology. He smiled as he remembered the one time he had seen his father truly angry with him. When he was twelve. In Yerushalayim.

Chapter 5

In Yeshua's twelfth year a majority of the families of Nazareth decided to celebrate Passover in Yerushalayim at his father's urging. It was to be a great encampment south of the holy city, near Bethlehem. Yosef was accustomed to the journey, as he and his growing family and some dozen villagers travelled in the spring almost every year for the annual feast. This year it would be special, a great encampment on the outskirts of the city of perhaps one hundred men, plus women and children. Yosef was to lead the way and make all the arrangements for tents and bedding and food.

For many of the villagers, the journey south would be the first time to behold the splendor of the new Temple constructed on the Temple Mount by King Herod almost four decades earlier.

Yeshua had accompanied Yosef to the Temple several times. He particularly loved the porticos around the inner courts, where the men would pass to and fro, debating the meaning of particular sayings in the Law and the Prophets.

That special year in Yerushalayim, he was so caught up in the excitement of the scene that he had lagged behind after Passover on the morning of the last visit by the men of Nazareth. The Nazarenes had offered prayers and then rejoined their families in the space designated for women and young children in the Temple's outer precincts.

In the great crowd mulling about, he had met other awestruck Nazareth youth. As they finally rushed off to join their families, Yeshua had remained behind, promising to join them shortly. He had wanted to be part of the crowd for just a few minutes longer.

There was a spirited conversation off to the side involving two pilgrims from the south. A larger group quickly formed around them and a disputation about points of the Law ensued. In his excitement Yeshua completely forgot about his family and the scheduled departure time.

He spent the day exchanging views on holy matters. As darkness fell he moved with others to the sleeping area for pilgrims at one side of the outer courts. On the following morning he rose, excited for more conversation. He had lost all thought of his parents and the people from Nazareth. Three days passed in this manner.

As newcomers drifted into the circle around him each day, there was quiet derision from the younger men who had come to see this young bumpkin from the north.

"Nazareth," they murmured, proud of their Yerushalayim schooling. "Not exactly a center of learning, is it?" They laughed their soft laughs as they nudged one another. And most of them drifted on.

But some stayed for the give and take of profound holy reflection.

"Come hear this child from Nazareth," word from the older men went around. "He is a prodigy of wisdom. Truly a blessing from the Lord!"

Yeshua was involved in an exchange with one of the older rabbis, the one with wise eyes, early in the morning of the fourth day when he suddenly saw his father striding toward him. As he saw the dark thundercloud in Yosef's face, he realized with a shock that he had completely forgotten all the Nazarenes and the departure for home.

Yosef waded through the circle of men around Yeshua and gave him a hard shake.

"Your mother and I have been searching high and low for you. And here you are, when we thought you had been eaten by wild animals!"

"Father, forgive me. I completely forgot."

Still holding his son, Yosef looked around at the circle of men. "We were with the Galilean encampment—a large group of people of Nazareth. I believed my son was with the other youth, and only after two day's journey did I realize he was nowhere to be found. What happened?"

Several men drifted away, not wishing to be part of an acrimonious reunion. But the wise-eyed man spoke quietly.

"We thought he was staying each night with a relative. He has amazed us daily with his knowledge, which he surely must have learned from you, his father."

Oblivious to the remark, Yosef pulled Yeshua aside and growled at his son. "And you, young pup, what do you have to say, yes? Speak up!"

"I am in my father's house," Yeshua protested.

"How can you say such a thing!" Yosef gave his son a shake.

"I don't know. The words just came to me."

Yosef stared at his son. He loosened his hold and walked several steps away. When he turned back he spoke in a calmer voice.

"Come, son. Your mother and the family are waiting." He gestured toward the outer courts, where the women and children were allowed during the day. "I do not wish her to worry for one moment longer."

Yosef nodded goodbye to the older man. He and Yeshua hurried to the pillared entryway. Miriam stood there, wringing her hands. She rushed to meet them, ignoring the frowns of men in the inner courts. She gave him a fierce hug and then pulled back.

"Child, why have you treated us like this! Your father and I have searched everywhere for you. How anxious we have been!"

Yeshua said to both parents, "Why were you searching for me? Didn't you know I must be in my father's house?"

Miriam loosened her hold and looked at Yosef.

"The words just came to him", he said. Yosef shrugged. He turned to Yeshua. "Come, son. It is time to go home."

They turned and started off through the crowded area. Some of the bystanders regarded them quizzically.

Miriam walked behind her husband and son, ignoring the looks. She was pondering Yeshua's words. She stopped and turned to look back at the inner courts where he had been safe all the time they searched for him. She turned around and ran to catch up with the others. Her eyes were filled with wondering.

Chapter 6

The shop door creaked on its hinges as it swung open part way, awaking Yeshua from his reverie. He shook his head to clear the memories of the long ago trip. Yehudah peered in at his two oldest brothers. "How are things in the toy shop?"

"Go away, brother," growled Yaakob. "Men are working."

"Of course! And to which wealthy merchant do we owe thanks for this particular delight?"

Yaakob lifted the plane he was using in his young brother's direction.

"Those who put food on our table are not to be mocked."

"Oh, pardon. Perhaps you will allow me to borrow one of your fine wheels to roll about in the street."

"Hold on, hold on, you two," warned Yeshua. He had stopped his own work and gazed speculatively at Yehudah.

"I think you are ready to join our work. Why don't you come apprentice with us? Begin by keeping the count of supplies needed for projects in the bins and on the shelves. Sweep up at the end of day. Make sure the tools are stored properly."

Yaakob snorted.

"Indoor work!" sneered Yehudah. "I'd rather work in the fields. Overseer of the shepherds of our flocks is what I call real work. They need overseeing. They're as stupid as the sheep."

"Ba-a-a-a," replied Yaakob.

"Stop it now, both of you," Yeshua commanded. "Yehudah, what prompts this interruption?"

"Our kinsman Yohannon has arrived, wilder-eyed then ever." Yehudah pinched his nose, and laughed. "Bringing with him such a rankness of stink that he must have forgotten to bathe for a week or more." He turned his head and sniffed loudly. "Ah, I smell him coming now."

He retreated, closing the door. They heard his voice greeting their kinsman and a rap on the door, followed immediately by its opening.

"Cousins! Greetings to you in the name of the Lord Most High!"

Yaakob grunted and turned back to his work, but Yeshua lay down his tool and crossed the room to embrace Yohannon.

As he drew back, Yeshua grimaced. "Kinsman, a good bath would make you more welcome as a guest."

"Ah, straightforward as ever!" Yohannon laughed. "Until three days ago I was as sweet-smelling as any bride might wish her groom to be. I have kept company with the Essenes in the wilderness. So intent on purification! Not satisfied with washing their hands before eating, they bathe before every meal in special pools! My flesh was in danger of becoming wrinkled by so much physical application of cleansing."

"Should have stayed," muttered Yaakob, his eyes surveying the even smoothness of his plane on a long piece of wood.

Yohannon turned to him. "No, as the days passed I realized that my way of holiness must take a different path. More cleansing of the heart and less of the body. At any rate, I have a bath awaiting me at the local inn before enjoying a wonderful meal with all my Nazareth kin. I wanted to waste no time in bringing greetings from my mother and our sorrow at the death of your father. I understand that he did not suffer overlong."

"Long enough," said Yaakob as Yohannon continued. "Yeshua, I have important matters about which I wish to speak with you. Perhaps a walk in the garden after supper?"

Yeshua smiled. "Yes, as long as you practice physical cleansing before the meal."

Chapter 7

After supper a well-bathed Yohannon retired to the garden with Yeshua. The garden, a long rectangle of land, was shared with the family whose house adjoined it at the far end. The garden consisted of fruit trees, olive trees and long rows of spring vegetables. Wooden benches were placed beneath three of the trees and the two men found their way to the bench that shielded them best from the warm glow of the setting sun.

"So, kinsman," Yeshua broke a brief silence in which they both contemplated the beauty and the bounty of the garden, "what has brought you to the north?"

Yohannon's eyes danced as he turned, "You have not changed! Well, I will get to the point. First, your mother's cousin, after whom your sister is named, is in declining health. She has attained an age of eighty years, blessed be the mercies of the Lord, and she has given me messages of condolence to bear to your mother."

"You are her only child. If these are her final days, why have you left her?"

"The wives of priests who remember my father Zechariah are attending to her. She is well cared for. And I expect to return home before she passes to our Lord's heavenly kingdom."

"But this talk of going to the Essenes. Surely you knew of her condition?"

"Yeshua, sometimes there are more important things than family."

"I cannot imagine."

Yohannon gazed at the garden and smiled. "I think you will."

Yeshua looked at him and spoke sternly. "With my father's sudden passing I am responsible for this household. I cannot imagine forsaking my mother. And you! You have no brothers or sisters as I do."

"Following the path that the Lord has set for me is the highest responsibility."

"Have you forgotten the admonition of the Law? Honor your father and your mother."

Yohannon was quiet for a moment and then spoke. "I have wrestled with it. The will of the Lord is an even higher admonition."

"And you, a mere mortal, presume to know the specific will of the Lord?"

"Kinsman, I walk about as you do; I sleep and eat and my bowels move. Yes, I am mortal."

"What then? Are you at last decided on following in your father's steps and training for the Temple priesthood?"

"No, Yeshua. I revere the memory of my father but I will not follow his path. At least, not in the Temple." Yohannon shifted on the bench and looked directly at Yeshua as he continued.

"I know from past conversations that you are a person of great insight and wisdom. Even the Essenes know of you." He smiled. "Mention of your name as my kinsman helped my entry into their community."

Yohannon became serious. "Now I will tell you why I speak as I do. But first, a question. Do you have visions?"

Yeshua almost laughed at the question but he saw that Yohannon was serious. "No. My father had holy dreams. I, too, have dreams, some of them very strange and vivid indeed. But I regard them as phantoms of my mind, brought on by overwork or its converse, concern about whether we again will find customers for our work when times are slow."

"How is the work these days?"

"Very good. We have a backload of orders. Yaakob and I are catching up for the time lost at my father's passing. Today we finished items of furniture and began the assembly of a new cart."

"I am glad for you. But let me return to myself. Of late I have visions. Not dreams, but rather things I see in the course of a day, as though suddenly a familiar place is bathed in radiant light and I discern something behind what is in place in front of me."

Yeshua smiled. "Perhaps you also are overworked at times, or worried, and your 'visions' give you relief from the press of daily affairs."

"No, no. They can be very real indeed." He paused, considering. "I will tell you in truth about my most recent vision. It came a week past while I was with the Essenes. One day, while yet again purifying myself in the room of the pool—before the midday meal as I recall—suddenly the far wall was transformed into a mist. As I watched, stupefied, the mist quieted and I saw myself standing in the middle of a river. People of all sorts lined the banks on both sides. There were priests of the Temple in impressive garments; there were women of high degree in their finery and also women in simple clothing of house or farm; and there were shepherds and fishmongers and merchants."

"Quite a sight, kinsman."

"Indeed. But there was more. In my own voice I was speaking loudly to them. 'In the wilderness prepare the way of YAHWEH, make straight in the desert a highway for our God.'"

Yeshua sucked in a great breath. "You dare to use the Holy Name? Take care! When the holy scrolls are read aloud in the synagogue, 'Lord' is always substituted."

"But it was not I here and now who was speaking," protested Yohannon. "It was I in the vision."

"A thin difference," replied Yeshua. "It is still sacrilege."

"Wait, there is more." Yohannon's voice throbbed with excitement. "In the vision I cried out with a loud voice, 'The glory of YAHWEH shall be revealed, all the people shall see it together, for the mouth of YAHWEH has spoken.'"

Yeshua rose and moved to the other end of the bench. "This is blasphemy!"

"No. The prophet Isaiah's words," Yohannon noted primly.

"Indeed," Yeshua replied through pursed lips. "I am quite familiar with Isaiah's words."

Yohannon nodded and smiled. "Yes. You are noted for your knowledge of scripture."

"Enough of your flattery. Besides your irreverent use of the Holy Name, were there other happenings in this tale of a vision?"

"I spoke more words from the prophet. Many more. Then the mist swirled and faded away and it was simply the wall of the room again. Exhausted as if by some great exertion, I fell backwards into the pool. Those who were near me lifted me up quickly. I questioned them discreetly for fear that they would think me crazed but they had seen nothing except my collapse."

He glanced at Yeshua. "I tell you truly."

"In this place with the Essenes. Had you been fasting?"
"No."

"Were you taken by a fever in the days before?"
Yohannon shook his head.

"Long walks of meditation in the heat of the desert?"

Another headshake.

Yeshua sighed. "Had any event prompted this vision? Word from your mother? A visitor?"

"None of that," Yohannon replied. "But there is more. At first I was troubled by what had happened. Like you, I thought the desert air might have prompted the vision.

"After a sleepless night I sought out the leader and told him I had decided to withdraw and return to my mother. He agreed, and that very morning I set off."

"Going to Yerushalayim?" Yeshua asked.

"That was my intention. By the river route to avoid bandits on the roads. I reached Nehar ha Yarden and followed it south. And then I saw something amazing." He paused and his face brightened as he looked at Yeshua.

"Another vision?"

"No, no. Even better! In those parts the great river is never wide except in the floods of early spring. I was able to make my way along the top of the river's bank."

"And?"

"Yeshua! I came round a bend and there it was! The very site I had seen in my vision the day before!"

Yeshua was silent for a moment. "Crowds of people waiting?"

"No, no. The river only. I pulled up my garments and almost fell in my haste to scramble down the bank and into the water. I tell you, it was the exact place. Instantly I changed my plans. I came north to Galilea to tell you and others of this."

Yeshua smiled. "You did smell of the river when you arrived here."

"Not an Essene model! Days of walking and brief sleep each night in the fields."

"Saving what dinars you have," Yeshua nodded. "Well, a good bath always will await you in Nazareth. But why did you not return to your mother first? Why the haste?"

Yohannon stood suddenly and took a few steps down the path to the house. He turned, and his voice was filled with passionate emotion.

"Yeshua, the time has come to prepare for the Messiah!"

Yeshua smiled at his kinsman's sudden fervor. "Yes, yes, but the days of the Maccabees are long past, if a revolt is what you have in mind."

Yohannon waved a hand. "No military uprising. What I have seen in my vision is a cleansing of the spirit. A return in our time to humbler, simpler ways. Herod is gone and this Roman, Pontius Pilate, who rules over central Palestine, cares little for matters of faith as long as we fork over the taxes that pay for the legions who maintain the peace."

Calmly Yeshua replied. "Herod's son Antipas rules over Galilee. Our taxes go mostly to pay for his grand new buildings in Tiberias and elsewhere."

"And also to Rome."

"And to people in Nazareth like my family, who make furniture for some of the new buildings and the homes of administrators and centurions."

"That is good for you." Yohannon began to wave his arms about as his voice rose. "But at least your life is not filled with pretension of the sort that is an unholy aroma in the streets of Yerushalayim, even unto the inner sanctums of the Temple itself!"

"Kinsman, calm yourself." Yeshua patted the bench. "Come and sit with me so that we may discuss your plan for purification. Or have the baths of the Essenes pickled your mind?"

Yohannon came and sat. He spoke passionately. "It is time to prepare. I go tomorrow to other villages in Galilea to find disciples who will assist me."

"But Galilea is unknown territory to you, a man of Yerushalayim."

"Some of the Essenes, men of the north, were in sympathy with me. They gave me names of those in Galilea who are of like mind. I am counting on a spiritual hunger that the Lord has created among these villagers. A holy yearning for a new day—the day of the Messiah."

"Are you serious? The Holy One, anointed of the Lord?"

"Yes. He is coming now. It has been revealed to me."

"Kinsman, again you border on sacrilege! Time for the Messiah! How can this be?"

"He is coming," insisted Yohannon. "It has been revealed to me. I am to prepare his way and I will anoint him!"

Chapter 8

"Let us calm ourselves," Yeshua said evenly. "You speak to me of a vision and what it means to you. You tell me that you have been chosen to anoint the Messiah."

Yohannon began to sputter, and Yeshua held up a hand. "You are filled with zeal."

"Yes! He is coming!"

"Even so, this journey to Galilea to recruit disciples may be misguided. You are a southerner. In the north, we are simpler folk than your family and friends in Yerushalayim. In our lives common sense and daily routine are treasured. Excited talk about the Messiah may result in ridicule and yawns rather than enthusiasm. And we have no Roman like Pilate ruling directly over us to rouse our religious convictions. For us, other than taxes for his new construction in Tiberias and the lavish parties within his circle, Antipas rules with a light hand."

"A hand of wickedness!"

"Oh, come now." Yeshua smiled. "All earthly rulers have their faults."

"Faults? You speak as though they were minor sins against heaven. Have you not heard how Philip, weak brother of Antipas, was divorced by his wife—*by his wife*—and she promptly married Antipas, that fox, as soon as he divorced *his* wife, the Nabatean princess. Disgusting! And the parties you speak of are orgies of the basest sort. Yet Antipas declares he is a follower of the Lord!"

"The fox, as you call him, will not be ignorant of your attempt at recruiting Galileans."

"I will be gone to a safe place on the river by then. My disciples will come with me."

"But where? Is the site in your vision within Pilate's rule? He seeks calm and steady payment of taxes. He certainly won't tolerate your preaching of purity and repentance! It will stir people up."

"Ah, Yeshua. That is how I know the vision is true and that I am the one called to this mission. The river site is not in an area Pilate rules. It is farther north on the river, in Perea."

Yeshua leaned forward. "I am astonished again. Perea is ruled by your fox, Antipas. How can you call it safe?"

Johannon smiled. "Because it is near the border of the Nabatean king, whose daughter Antipas abruptly and cruelly divorced and ejected from Galilea. She has returned to her father in Nabatea. Antipas has little stomach for war, but in Nabatea vengeance is a strong potion slowly sipped. Antipas has no wish for a high profile in Perea. It would be regarded as hostile and provocative. Besides, the Roman legion based in Perea has no desire for such a provincial spat. Thanks to the wisdom of the Lord, I will outfox the fox!"

"Your vision . . . if you succeed in bringing it to life, will you follow the way of the Essenes?"

"No. *Their* way is to withdraw. They forbid contact with any man who has not proven his commitment to their way of the Lord. I wish them well, but their way is not my way."

"Yet they welcomed you, son of a priest."

Yohannon nodded. "I went to them as a learner. One who has good credentials, including your kinship. But a man is not fully welcomed until commitment is proven. It takes a year, at the least."

"Why did you go to them in the first place?"

"Because the ways of the priests have become an abomination in my eyes and the eyes of the Lord. I do not speak as the priests do, asking for gifts to the Temple that never reach the poor and needy. The Sadducees who are custodians of the Temple Mount care nothing for simplicity of dress but instead wear sumptuous garments which make their superior position and their self-centered holiness clear to all whom they meet in the streets and byways of Yerushalayim. They even have adopted Roman customs like reclining on elegant couches at their dinners instead of sitting upright as honest men do. Their *true* interest is not the holiness of the people but rather their own political advancement and financial success.

"Further, they are in alliance with the moneychangers—" He stopped. "One example. First, a question. Other than the priests on duty and the guards, who are most of the people who worship at the Temple?"

Yeshua thought. "Certainly not the wealthy. Simple people from Yerushalayim and the villages."

Yohannon clapped his hands and laughed. "Without a doubt! Now let me tell you what has happened in recent years. Let's say you are not a prosperous carpenter but a poor yet pious man, perhaps a worker on an estate."

"All right, let's suppose."

"What is the very lowest sacrifice to the Lord such a man can make?"

"Two pigeons," replied Yeshua.

"Exactly. Two pigeons. At what cost?"

Yeshua calculated. "Today—probably one dinar, possibly two."

"You are a long time away from Yerushalayim, friend." Yohannon laughed again, a bitter sound.

"More, I suppose. How much?" asked Yeshua, intrigued with this picture of life in the holy city.

"Twenty dinars."

"This cannot be!" Yeshua exclaimed.

"Ah, but it is." Yohannon gave him a twisted smile. "Twenty pieces of silver. Ten for each pigeon."

"But that, that's unbelievable!" Yeshua sputtered.

"The Sadducees have an arrangement with the money changers. The money changers kick back a pittance to the pigeon breeders."

"Shame upon the Sadducees!" exclaimed Yeshua. "And the money changers must be evicted from the holy places!"

"Of course," answered Yohannon. "But first we must have a widespread change of the spirit. The whole business is rotten. The Sadducees give obeisance to the Pharisees, but the joint council, the Sanhedrin, is a nest of vipers, writhing and coiling so as to outdo one another."

"Take care," Yeshua warned. "We in the north follow the way of the Pharisees."

"So I have heard. Yet they also have faults. With eyes lifted to heaven they preach piously of following the holiness of the Law in every jot and tittle, thus entwining themselves in the thickets of the most rigid precepts. In doing so, they become pompous, presumptuous and prideful. They have forgotten the helpful corrections and warnings of the Prophets of old."

"A harsh judgment," said Yeshua.

Yohannon grimaced. "It is all politics in the end. The chief priest, Caiphas, is appointed by Pontius Pilate, so do not look to your precious Pharisees for anything that might roil the Romans."

"But they do observe the Law!" Yeshua protested.

His kinsman laughed. "You last went to Passover in Yerushalayim when?"

"A number of years ago. Perhaps ten or more."

"Yet your father Yosef took such joy in going to Yerushalayim before then. Your family often met with mine in joyous celebration. Why did he stop his pilgrimage?"

Yeshua sighed. "My father regarded himself as prosperous and tithed in the synagogue with thanksgiving to the Lord. He also knew a great deal about the Law. In recent years he was disturbed by stories of persons standing on the street corners of Yerusalayim, praying loudly with a multitude of high-sounding phrases. And tales that those who gave alms would hire a man to go before them to blow a trumpet at their offering, so that everyone around would know what great things had been done."

"And what did your father say about such doings?"

"He called them hypocrites who put on a great show but no one knew what irreligious acts they committed in private." Yeshua smiled at a sudden memory. "And he lectured us all from childhood onward about the false inequalities that men devise. He drummed it into our heads that we all are children of the Lord."

"Precisely. And that is why I have been called by the Lord. It is a time for renewal of the faith of our fathers so that we truly can be a light to the nations, as the prophet said. Men of low rank and high, working together in common purpose to restore true holiness and humility among our people. Very soon now, the Messiah will come among us to restore the Kingdom of David forever."

"You truly believe you have been called?"

"Yes. Called to offer the ancient rite of baptism at the site of my vision to all who will come out from the cities and farms to pledge a commitment to new life. Now is the coming of the Messiah and we must be ready—yes, even in Yerushalayim!"

"Calm yourself, kinsman. Tell me again how you know of your call."

"The vision, for one. Clues and hints over the years. Lately I have learned about the beginning."

Yohannon stood again and paced a few steps along the path and turned back, looking directly at Yeshua. "As you know, my father Zechariah was a priest in the Temple. He and my mother Elisheva had no child. Year after year, no child. She has spoken to me in my adulthood, after my father died, of how shamed she felt, as though the barrenness was visited upon her because of something one of her ancestors had done or failed to do. And then, in her forty-ninth year, she conceived." He smiled. "Me."

"I know this," said Yeshua. "My mother has told me of her visit to her cousin, your mother, and of how glad they were together, for my mother also was with child." And Yeshua smiled. "Me."

CHAPTER 9

YOHANNON NODDED. "HAVE YOU heard of what happened to my father during that time?"

"Something about an illness that rendered him mute," Yeshua replied.

"Ha! Much better than that! It was the common reason given out. But my mother recently related to me what he told her after his speech was restored.

"It was his priestly duty to tend to the altar of perpetual incense. One day he looked up from his prayers at the altar and beheld a man in a brilliant white robe standing beside him. He was frightened, because this intruder was a terrible violation of Temple law. The man told him that his name was Gabriel, a messenger from the Lord. He had come to tell my father that his wife would bear a son who would prepare the people for the coming of the Messiah."

"Ah!" Yeshua exclaimed. "And did Zechariah believe this—this vision?"

"No, and that is a lesson for me. The messenger rendered him speechless because Zechariah laughed in disbelief and shed bitter tears, thinking his wife was beyond childbearing years. After my birth, he told my mother he had thought at first the messenger was a cruel joke by a younger priest so as to shame him."

"Oh, my."

"Indeed." Yohannon continued. "Now for the interesting part. Because of his disbelief, the messenger rendered him mute but he also told Zechariah his speech would be restored when the child was born. And he said the child should be given the name, 'Yohannon.'"

"And so you were."

"You do know what's odd about that? The name."

"The whole story is odd," reflected Yeshua.

"But it is the truth!"

"Very well. Enlighten me about the name."

Yohannon gave him a look. "Perhaps you are not so bright as your reputation has it."

"No doubt. But continue."

"My father and mother both came from priestly families with a wealth of venerable names to choose from, yes? And if not one of them, the name of my father. Surely there would be no more children after my blessed birth, so what better name than Zechariah?"

"It would seem suitable."

Yohannon paused and gave Yeshua a long look. "Do you not see some similarity in our situations?"

Yeshua started to say something but Yohannon waved him silent.

"You prefer plain talk, so here it is. Why are you, like me, not named for your father, Yosef? Or Seraiah, to honor your mother's father?"

"My father was a righteous man, who gave me a righteous name. Yeshua. The meaning he preferred for the name is 'The Lord is my salvation.'"

"Yeshua. A godly name though not uncommon. Why, there is in central Palestine even a robber of pilgrims named Yeshua Barabbas."

Yeshua raised a hand to strike Yohannon, but a firm voice within him said, *Do not.* His hand fell to his lap as he muttered, "You defame my father!"

"I see you are angry. Forgive me. All I am saying is neither you nor I are named for our fathers."

"It does happen," protested Yeshua.

"Of course. of course," Yohannon soothed. "But it *is* an interesting coincidence within your mother's family. She was pregnant with you when she came south to be with my mother, who was even greater with child. I am sure the two of them had a great deal to talk about. The older woman and the younger. First child for both. Has she ever mentioned anything about those days?"

Yeshua was calmer now. "No. She returned, she has told me, and then it was the time of the census for the new taxes levied afterwards. All families were to go to the birthplace of their father's ancestor, so my parents went to Bethlehem. I was born there, actually. A difficult birth, my mother has said. A kinswoman of my father was midwife. She and my father laughed in recent years about those hard times after they had enjoyed a glass of wine here in the garden." He looked up at Yohannon. "They were both usually so serious. It was pleasant to hear them murmuring and leaning against each other. It was as if they were young again."

Yohannon waved his hand. "I suspect there was more to tell. To tell *you*. It is only lately that my mother related the strange tale connected with my birth. At the end of the telling, she made me promise that if I ever travelled to Galilea, I was to come to Miriam and say she was to tell you about the old stories. In my last days with the Essenes, I received a message from mother about Yosef's passing. She is not able to travel now, and she asked specifically if I might visit here and after expressing our sorrow, to tell Miriam to speak to you 'about the old stories.'"

"Strange," Yeshua mused, "my father said much the same in his last words to us all."

"So!" The other man clapped his hands. "Coincidences abound—or they are the working of the Lord. And now the real purpose of my visit."

Yeshua smiled. "At last."

"No, no. This is serious and I want you to hear me out."

"Go on."

Yohannon spoke earnestly. "I will tell you with no embroidery. As I have said, I am called by the Lord to prepare the way for the Messiah. I now know that from my birth this is so."

"So you have said, kinsman. Several times."

"Yes, but I did not tell you fully of my vision in the pool of the Essenes." He paused. "Another man was with me. That man is you."

Yeshua stared. "I do not understand your meaning."

The eyes of Yohannon glowed. "You are meant to carry out this mission with me. You will be my first disciple."

Yeshua sat stunned and then sputtered, "But how could I leave my mother—and all the work to be done that supports our household?"

"But what about the work that the Lord sets before you? I saw you clearly in my vision! The two of us standing in the river. Yaakob can carry on the work here. From the little I have seen, I think he may even be a better carpenter than you. No offense, Yeshua, but he has done the more difficult parts—the cart wheels, for example. And the decorative panels for the chests and all the rest."

"You are a keen observer," smiled Yeshua. "Yaakob indeed is more talented than I. But he is rough around the edges when it comes to the matter of dealing with the buyers."

"He can learn, kinsman. And your other brothers—they quickly can learn under his supervision, though I suspect he is a strict taskmaster. Your mother will not suffer any loss in income."

"This vision of yours!" Yeshua spoke angrily. "No, no. In Nazareth it would be a shameful thing for the oldest son to behave in such a manner. Yosef had no brother to look after her interests. She herself said to me on the night my father died, 'You are the head of the household.' Besides, there are my sisters to consider. Elisheva is of marrying age, and Rebekah is not far behind. There are serious negotiations to be made. Father and I spoke about a certain man in the village who would be a suitable match. Father knew he had the savings to do it."

"Words, words, words." Yohannon threw up his hands. "You describe things that bind us to our earthly ways. What about the ways of our heavenly father? I tell you truly, it was clearly you that I saw in my vision. Come with me. A new day is dawning. Together we will prepare the way."

Yeshua rose from the bench. "You speak with passion. Yet no decision as important as this can be made in the heat of the moment. I will think over what you have said and give you my answer in the morning."

"No." Yohannon also rose and stood close. "I saw you clearly. At the river. With me. I stake my life on it. The Lord wants you to be with me at the coming of the Messiah. You are meant to do this!"

His eyes fierce, Yohannon spoke evenly yet firmly. "I will leave from the inn at the first cock crow. Give me your assent now. You can join me in a week or so, but Yeshua, I want your answer now!"

"Very well. A moment."

Yeshua turned and walked away from Yohannon onto the pathway around the garden. He walked slowly, surveying the flourishing vegetables that his sisters had planted. He sought calm in his spirit.

The passion of his kinsman was clear. Yohannon's vision seemed true, apart from his impudence, but it found no resonance in Yeshua's heart. Despite his own words about family responsibilities, he did not wish to thwart the call of the Lord. Was the message of Yohannon to be his own?

As he walked, the first words of a favorite Psalm from King David of old filled his mind. *I will give thanks to the Most High with all my heart; I will tell of your wonderful deeds. I will be glad and exult in you, I will sing praise to your name, O Lord.*

He sighed. The mission his kinsman described sounded more like a hammer of judgment rather than joyful praises.

He stopped and turned. He looked along the pathway and lifted his eyes to Yohannon, thirty steps away, gazing back at him with uplifted jaw and clenched lips. Awaiting his reply.

The evening was still and it seemed that the world was hushed around him. Sudden warmth filled his heart and his tense muscles relaxed. He heard again the quiet voice within. *Do not go. It is not yet time.*

He smiled at his kinsman and walked back to him.

"Good." Yohannon returned his smile. "You will go with me and together we shall accomplish great things preparing the way for the Messiah."

"No." Yeshua spoke firmly. "I cannot deny your vision but there must be another meaning for my presence in it. I wish you well, but I will remain here."

Anger reddened Yohannon's face. "Very well. You have made your choice. I will be away early. If you change your mind I will be at the inn." He turned and stalked to the gate that led to the street. He banged it noisily shut behind him and was gone.

Chapter 10

Three days passed. Nothing had been heard as yet of Yohannon's recruiting efforts in Galilea. The cart was finished and Yeshua hitched it up to the family pony and rode to a neighboring hamlet for delivery to Ezra, a farmer.

He found the man to be in a foul mood. Few words were spoken as the farmer inspected the cart and its wheels and paid Yeshua the price that had been agreed. As Ezra turned to go into his house, Yeshua placed a hand on the man's shoulder.

"My friend, something is troubling you."

Ezra stood still for a moment and then turned. His face was contorted by sudden wrath.

"It is that thief, that crook, that slanderer Tobias!" he roared. Yeshua stepped backward in the face of the blast.

"But you are friends."

"No longer!"

"You both have lived here for years. You have traded implements back and forth for work in your respective fields. What on earth has happened?"

"Ah, you have not heard of this trespassing in Nazareth? Let me tell you then and you can pass along news of what this wretch has done." He began jabbing a forefinger into Yeshua's chest to emphasize his words. "Tobias the son of falsehood, Tobias the trickster, Tobias the trespasser."

Yeshua gently pushed the forefinger away. "What has brought on this fit of rage?"

"Rage? I'll show him rage, that conniver, that thief, that—"

"Ezra, you will make yourself ill with this anger! Please calm yourself and tell me what has happened."

The man opened his mouth to expel more epithets, but Yeshua waved him to silence.

Ezra took several deep breaths. "All right, I will tell you and then you will be as shocked as I was at the terrible thing he has done. The scoundrel!"

Yeshua waited.

"There is a field," Ezra waved a hand to the north, "which has been in my family for generations. A rocky place and it has lain fallow all these years."

He took a deep breath. "This spring I thought to myself, if the rocks are cleared, it might be suitable for wheat. And so I went to the field and cleared the rocks—no easy task, that was—and a week ago I returned to the field to prepare the ground for planting."

His rage began to build again. "And do you know who was there?"

"Tobias?"

"Yes! Standing there all pleased with himself and looking about. Well, I said to myself, what is this, that he is standing in *my field* with such a satisfied air. So I walked to him and said very nicely, 'Good day, friend Tobias. What brings you here?'"

"And the reply?"

"'Dear friend Ezra, are you the angel of the Lord who has cleared my field for me?'

"Well! I disabused him of the notion that the field is his and told him in no uncertain terms that the field was purchased by my great-grandfather."

He paused to catch his breath.

Yeshua quickly asked, "He definitely thought the field was his possession?"

"Oh, no question about it! The field had been purchased by *his* great-grandfather. 'Clear as the sky is blue,' he said. 'No, no,' I replied, 'I have heard stories about this field from my grandfather and my father.'

"His face flushed a dark red at that. 'You are mistaken. It has always been *my* ancestor in the story. I will be glad to settle with you for the favor of clearing the field so that now I may use it.'

"'I intend it for my use,' said I. 'You are welcome to visit me here in the spring planting because it is *my field*.'"

"'No, it is *mine*, trespasser!' he roared and turned to walk back to his donkey at the other end of the field. I tell you, Yeshua, such a rage was upon me that I started after him, intending to throw him to the ground and beat him, but the hand of the Lord restrained me and instead I turned and walked back to my own donkey."

"I am glad of that. Where do matters stand now?"

"I am waiting for him to come to his senses."

Yeshua sighed. "And he is likely thinking the same about you." He thought. "No papers? From years ago?"

"Of course not. The purchase was made, a handshake and the matter was done. You know this is the way we do such things—from the time of Abraham on."

"Yes. But let me get one thing clear. Your friend—" A guttural sound from Ezra. "Your *former* friend, Tobias. He clearly said that the field had been purchased by his great-grandfather?"

"Yes, the liar."

"Perhaps."

Yeshua fell silent for a moment. It was a terrible thing for two friends to have a falling out.

"You both have helped to make a minyan on holy days of prayer. You both now claim this field. You might go to the rabbi and seek his help in sorting out this property issue, but it appears that would mean only another shouting match with no resolution."

"Yes, yes, but the field is mine." An idea struck him. "Yeshua, you are known for your holy knowledge. Tobias respects you. If *you* were to go to him and show him the error of his ways, hmm?"

"As I have no pressing matters in Nazareth, I will go to Tobias today. But the matter will not easily be resolved now that there is so much anger on both sides."

"Yes, but you are eloquent of tongue. I am sure you can convince him."

A few moments later Yeshua departed from a smiling Ezra. Leading his pony, he walked to the house of Tobias.

He knocked at the door.

Perhaps he will not be at home, he hoped, and then felt ashamed of the thought.

The door opened and the wife of Tobias greeted him warmly.

"Yeshua! This is a blessing. Are you here with news of the synagogue?"

"No, just passing through on business. Is Tobias in?"

"It's that furor Ezra has started, isn't it?"

He nodded. She sighed.

"He's in the garden around in the back, expressing his anger mightily on the helpless vegetables. Shall I call him?"

"No. I'll go round."

Turning the corner of the house he saw and heard the truth of what she had said. The loud thumps of a hoe greeted him and he stood for a moment, watching Tobias as he attacked the weeds. Missing some, he decapitated several garden plants and swore at the damage.

"Tobias."

The man turned. His face was filled with a wrath as great as Ezra's had been, but it drained from his face as he saw his visitor.

"Yeshua! Thank the Lord! Just the person I want to see."

Holding the hoe, he walked over to Yeshua. "How is Miriam doing?"

"My mother is well, thank you."

"Good, good." Tobias eyed him. "Have you heard about this awful stink?"

"I delivered a new cart to Ezra and he delivered himself of a few choice comments."

Tobias leaned on his hoe. "How that man can claim property that's been in my family for years!"

"Hmm. I am surprised the issue has not arisen before."

"Well, in all truth, the field was covered by so many rocks that even sheep had a hard time with footing. But with the field mostly cleared, there were new possibilities. I looked it over and was thinking of a nice wheat crop. The soil is good."

"Ezra cleared the field?"

"Oh yes. The fellow who owns the next field over, he told me. Said it was wonderful to have a friend like that. I was so glad to see Ezra in the field the other day. I was ready to compensate him well for all his hard labor. But then his mouth opened, spewing venomous lies."

"And you had no hint previously of Ezra's claim?"

"None at all. We never spoke of it. I thought the field pretty much worthless, you see."

"I am glad you have a deed of some sort."

"Nonsense. The deed was in the handshake between the previous owner and my great-grandfather." He eyed

Yeshua. "We're simple folk here but always trustworthy up until now."

Yeshua was quiet. In his heart he was offering up a silent prayer. *Heavenly father, all the land belongs to you. Praise be to you that you loan it to us mortals for our use. Help me with these two obstinate men!* An idea occurred to him.

"I'd like to see the field."

"Be my guest. As a matter of fact, it's off to the right on the road to Nazareth. Can't miss it. Rocks piled at one end and the other. I told him I'd pay him, but he just stomped off."

"I'll ride out there. I'd like you to meet me there and we can look things over."

"Gladly."

"Oh, and on my way, I'll stop at Ezra's house. I want him to meet me there also."

"The two of us? Together at the field I own?"

"Yes."

Tobias snorted. "What's the use of that?"

"I have an idea."

Chapter 11

A SHORT WHILE LATER Yeshua was engaged in a tour of the field before the two antagonists arrived. He urged his pony up one side and down the other. He looked at the piles of rocks at either end. He smiled as his eyes noticed the old tree at the edge of the field, halfway between the two rock piles at opposite ends. He turned and saw the two embittered contestants walking toward him, scowling, on either side of the dirt road. He swung down from the pony and greeted them as they approached.

"Thank you for coming."

"Has he recognized his error?" both men asked at the same time, and then frowned at each other.

"Let's talk about this land."

Both men folded arms across their chests and pursed their lips.

"But not here by the rock pile," Yeshua said. "Walk with me to a place where we can view the whole field."

Leading the pony he walked onto the field and proceeded to the other end. Ezra and Tobias followed him. Halfway along, Yeshua stopped. They stopped.

"You have been good friends until now. True?"

They glared at each other and prepared to speak. He waved his hand to silence them.

"You have helped one another in your respective fields year after year. True?"

Reluctantly they nodded. "Yes, but—" Tobias began to say. A palm up from Yeshua.

"And now this terrible controversy over ownership has divided you. True?"

Both men nodded.

"Each man claiming ownership from the days of his great-grandfather. True?"

"But he—", sputtered Ezra, pointing at Tobias.

"Hold on," soothed Yeshua. "Tobias, do you truthfully claim that this land was purchased by your great-grandfather?"

"Absolutely, as the Lord is my witness."

"Ezra, do you truthfully claim that this land was purchased by your great-grandfather?"

"Of course! Why else would I have gone to all the trouble of clearing the field?"

"Ah, now. What if you both are telling the truth?"

They stared at him.

"In the story of ownership that came down to both of you, who was the seller of the land?"

"A man from—" replied Tobias.

"Nabatea." finished Ezra.

They looked at each other.

Yeshua smiled. "And I suppose that, having lived here for many years, he decided in his old age to return home."

"Yes," they said in unison. They looked at each other, for the first time without rancor.

"Clever men, those Nabateans," remarked Yeshua.

"But I am sure he sold it first to my ancestor!" Ezra exclaimed.

"No, to mine," Tobias stated firmly.

Yeshua smiled. "Why don't you take this tale of 'who first?' to the regional council. You both are members. I am sure that the other farmers will be sympathetic to one or the other of you."

They stood silent, contemplating the council, composed of their peers.

"They'd hoot us out of the room," muttered Tobias.

"Well, then?"

"That rotten scoundrel," exploded Ezra.

Tobias laughed. "That's a good one! Both of our ancestors fooled into thinking they alone owned this field."

Ezra was grim-faced. "And our families both had other land. This rocky field was to be developed later, but later never came. Until I cleared the rocks out." He looked around. "Most of them."

"Now," Yeshua said, "let me tell you an old, old story. In the days of King Solomon a child was born. But this happy event was marred by two mothers who came before the king, each loudly claiming to be the true mother and crying for justice. The king thought and thought and then rendered his decision. He told the mothers that a swordsman would cut the child in two and give half to each mother. Of course the mother who truly was the mother pleaded with the king, sobbing and crying, not to do such a thing but rather to give the whole child to the other woman. Solomon's threat worked, and the child was reunited with his true mother, and the other woman was sent into exile."

Bewildered, both men stared at him. At last Tobias spoke.

"I do not take your meaning, Yeshua."

"You can do what Solomon could not." He gestured to each end of the field. "You are standing in the middle of the field. Both of you have considered the other a trespasser." He pointed toward the old tree. "By the grace of the Lord, that venerable tree marks the exact middle of the field. Walk straight across that middle to this side of the field and rocks from the work of Ezra could be used as markers."

"But this truly is my field," Ezra murmured petulantly.

"Yes. And also the field of Tobias. Both of you are owners, victims of a sly Nabatean out to double his money decades ago."

"I see where you're going with this story," said Tobias. "And I do not agree. The field belongs to me."

"A fair division. Forgive each other your trespasses."

"No!" the two men shouted in unison.

"No? You both are fiercely angry at each other when the anger should be directed at the cunning Nabatean. But that seems unsatisfactory and unjust. I understand. Now let me tell you another story that begins here, today, and extends into the future. Your anger with each other continues. Like a poisoned well, it will affect everyone around you. Eventually you, or your sons, or the sons of your sons will lash out in vengeance. What then? The other family retaliates. There will be maimings and even murders. Is that the legacy you wish to bequeath to your grandchildren and the ones who come after them? Think carefully now."

They were silent and stony-faced, both staring at the ground.

"Well?" Yeshua asked. "Which future do you want—peace? Or everlasting enmity between your families?"

Yeshua held his breath. There was a long and profound silence before they looked up from the ground to meet the eyes of Yeshua.

"Peace," both answered glumly.

Yeshua expelled his breath. "Let us thank the Lord, from whom the gift of common sense comes! Now, here's a thought. When I spoke to each of you separately, you both had the same idea for the use of this field."

Ezra turned to Tobias. "You were thinking of planting wheat next year?"

"Yes. And you?"

"The best crop for the field. Our field. We do not need to divide it."

"Agreed."

"We will work it together and our sons and grandsons after us."

Tobias sighed. "I am still indebted to you for clearing the field. It is only fair for me to compensate you."

"No, no, my friend," exclaimed Ezra. "It makes possible the work of both of us in *our* field. Your debt is forgiven!"

The two men gave a great whoop of laughter and embraced.

When at last they turned to thank him, Yeshua was headed toward Nazareth on his pony.

CHAPTER 12

AFTER SUPPER THE NEXT day, Miriam turned to Yeshua. "We need to fill several water jugs for the morning. Strong arms would help. Yeshua, will you go with me?"

"Yes, of course." At last, he thought, she is ready for our conversation.

But his mother said nothing as they walked side by side to the town well, Yeshua carrying the two large water vessels.

"Let us sit on the bench and rest ourselves," she said as they reached the well, encircled by a worn wooden bench made by Yosef years before.

Yeshua set down the water vessels and sat beside her. She looked about. The square was empty.

"We are early. Soon others will come, but not yet." She gave him a sideways glance. "Our kinsman made a noisy departure. Did you argue?"

"A disagreement."

"What was it that angered him so?"

"He wanted something I could not give."

"I am only your mother, so of course there is no need for me to know."

Her eyes flashed. He smiled.

"You need fish no longer, Mother. Your cousin Elisheva is gravely ill yet he had gone away to spend time with that desert community. The holy ones at Qumran known as Essenes."

"Oh. But what angered him so?"

"He wanted me to do something of the same. Join him as a disciple in public purification rites at Bethabara, the place of fording on the Yarden. My response was that I have responsibilities here, and he left in a huff."

"Cousin Elisheva." She sighed. "I suppose I should go to her."

"He said the wives of priests were tending to her. We need you here."

"Oh." Her voice trailed off and she took a deep breath before continuing. "Did he say anything else about his mother?"

"A number of things. He spoke of his mother telling him about the time you both were with child and you went to be with her."

"A strange subject. Years and years ago."

"He wished to unburden himself of it."

"It seemed the thing to do. I helped her with his birth." She fell silent.

"And he told me of what I had not heard before—how his father was struck mute after conversation with a strange visitor. And how he was given a name not known in the family history. He is convinced that it is no coincidence that he and I were given names not in our lineage." He lifted a hand and gently turned her face to his. "Mother, I have cast *my* net down but no fish have been caught. Let us now speak plainly. What is it you are to tell me?"

Her eyes filled with tears. "It is a troublesome matter."

Yeshua sighed. "Neither father nor you have ever talked with me about that time. He is gone, and if you do not tell me before you join him, I will never know the answer to this mystery."

"It is about a time that was both wonderfully glorious and also terribly frightening."

"When I was a child?" Yeshua asked.

"No. Before you were born." She stared at the ground.

"Mother, at times you can be quite exasperating!"

"Very well." Miriam wiped her eyes with a sleeve. "Yosef was a kind man, a godly man, and a good husband and father."

"That is how I knew him, mother. Now, the mystery of the old stories?"

She patted his hand and held it in hers on the bench as she turned her gaze away from him. "Let me start from the beginning so that you can better understand what happened later on.

"As you know, my father Seraiah was rabbi of the synagogue in Cana. He was devoted to his study of the Law and the Prophets and did not marry my mother until later in life. She also was older, but not as old as he. I was born soon after, their only child. My father was an only child. They hoped for more children but it was not to be. Of mother's family, only a younger brother remained. Cleopas. Her parents were both gone but her father left mother money for herself and Cleopas. Uncle Cleopas was a great help, but when I was young he moved here to Nazareth and took a wife. Mother helped with the bride-price he needed for his wife."

"Yes, yes," Yeshua said. "I know your family history."

"Yeshua, please. Remember what Yosef said that last night. It's *my* story. Let me tell it in my own way."

"Please do," he exclaimed.

She smiled at him. "Patience." She continued. "As a girl I learned not only the care of a house but also more worldly things. My father was quite progressive for his times. He held religious school for the boys, as rabbis do. He also formed one for the girls, twelve of us, and gave us nicknames from the Twelve Tribes. We learned about the Law and the Prophets as well as stories from our history. The

Patriarchs. Moshe and Yehoshua and the others. Mighty King David. The destruction of the Temple in Yerushalayim and the rebuilding. The great captivity. The revolts that arose and failed. And even some Greek—what a strange language compared to ours! But he said it was important for us as future wives to know how to do our sums and the names of things so that we could deal with the Greek traders in the weekly market."

"You truly were fortunate," said Yeshua. "I understand now why you have insisted on education for my sisters. And our father agreed with you. How did you meet Yosef?"

"Through Cleopas. Your grandfather began the carpentry shop but had grown to an age when he had difficulty with the tools. Mostly he sat in the garden and dozed. Cleopas told my parents that Yosef had taken over the shop and seemed quite an up-and-comer."

"Yes," Yeshua agreed. "And father was a skillful, patient teacher for myself, Yaakob, and Yosa in our apprenticeships. But do not stop."

"In my fifteenth year, I overheard a conversation between my parents. They were discussing a suitable match. Yosef of Nazareth. Twice as old as I he was, but well settled and financially prepared for marriage. A promising trade, carpentry. Although he was not a rabbi, he was considered quite knowledgeable in religious matters. My father had spoken to his father and there was a tentative agreement between them. But my mother said that old customs need not hold in the present age. Mother insisted that I meet him and give my consent. Father grumbled and sputtered, but in the end she had her way."

She fell silent, remembering.

"And you met him," prodded Yeshua.

"Oh yes." She laughed. "I must have seemed terribly prim and shy, but goodness, he was twice as old as I, which made him seem ancient, and he was such a sturdy man, though well spoken!"

"The betrothal agreement was made?"

"Not at first sight! My parents were eavesdropping behind the doorway curtain. Suddenly mother came bustling through and firmly suggested that we should take a walk though the village so that I might tell him of my homemaking skills."

"So much for not holding to old customs," Yeshua murmured.

She turned to Yeshua and smiled broadly. "Though she approved of father's class for young women, she feared that too much mention of my intellectual pursuits would put a damper on the betrothal.

"So he and I took our walk up one street of Cana and down another. I was careful to listen to his plans for expanding his work. I smiled and nodded most agreeably and mentioned nothing about the Law and the Prophets or history or Greek traders. And by the end of our walk I thought him to be a good and thoughtful man, so the plans for our betrothal were all right."

"I am delighted to hear of such wonderful things. It does not sound terrible at all!"

"That came soon after."

A long silence. Yeshua waited. She cleared her throat.

"The betrothal was announced in both Cana and Nazareth. The day afterwards my parents escorted me to the groom's house, as was the custom. There we met Yosef's elderly parents. It was a preliminary meeting. Once the details were settled by the two fathers I would be spending a great deal of time at their house. After the wedding feast, it would be our home as well as the home of Yosef's parents."

She paused. "My son, you have had no thoughts of marriage yet. But there are several men in the village who spoke to Yosef in general terms about the suitability of their daughters for you."

Yeshua stared at her. "I was not aware of this!"

"Of course not. Generalities abound until the circling conversation begins to hint at a positive result." She looked away, musing. "Now that Yosef is gone, and your Uncle Cleopas, I am not sure who is to make the arrangements for you." She looked at him. "As head of the house you will be in charge of these matters. Choosing someone who will be a good wife for each of your brothers and good husbands for your sisters. These are important arrangements and include negotiating the bride-price we will pay for the wives of your brothers. They will be joining us after the betrothal."

Yeshua was quiet, absorbing the information.

"I was fortunate," his mother continued. "Yosef's mother passed to her heavenly reward not long after our return to Nazareth."

"Your return to Nazareth?"

"Yes. After your birth. But back to arrangements."

"I have no memory of Yosef's mother."

"Thank the Lord," Miriam exclaimed. "It was only for a short while that I heard her many corrections of what I did, and how I did, and so on and so on. Accompanied by reminders of how fortunate I was to be married to Yosef."

"I know of some situations that are prickly," responded Yeshua.

"You have only to look around the synagogue, Yeshua. Fathers and sons are sitting together on one side. On the other, in the women's section, there are several wives who are bold enough to sit with their daughters apart from their husband's mothers. What does that tell you?"

"Some household situations are difficult, I know. But their husbands are generous."

"Ha! Wait until you will have to deal with our situation. Your wife will join us. Your brothers will marry and their wives will join us. It is wonderful to be together, but not too close. A year ago I spoke privately to Mishael the stonemason about the possibility of adding rooms onto the back of our house and above it." She emphasized her next words. "With solid doors, built in your workshop, to ensure privacy for all the families."

"We must trust in the Lord to provide for our harmony," Yeshua protested.

Miriam gave him a sweet smile. "Of course, my son. But back to my story."

"I want to hear about the return to Nazareth. From where?"

"Egypt," she said. "Please, may I continue?"

Yeshua nodded.

Chapter 13

"We met with Yosef's parents. They were thrilled that their son was to marry a rabbi's daughter, and my mother spoke quite positively about the treasure of household skills I would bring to their home. At the end of our conversation the two fathers were to settle on the bride-price and date for the marriage. Mother and I left them chatting and returned home.

"It was a warm spring evening. Father returned, happily humming about the arrangements that had been made. After the supper dishes were washed, I knew he and mother wanted to talk, so I told mother that I was going to sit in the garden for a bit of fresh air. Our garden was a lovely, peaceful place, well suited to collecting my thoughts. We had a small fountain at the center and beautiful blooming flowers all around.

"I sat on a bench near the gate and wondered what life with Yosef would bring. I knew that my parents loved me. We were very close. How would life be once I was living in Nazareth, separated from everything that home meant to me? There was my mother's easy humor and commonsense, my father's wisdom and instruction about the wider world, and, most of all, the wonderful stories I loved to hear about their own parents and grandparents. Some times I would sit for hours just listening to those stories. I never tired of them.

"Those days soon would end. What was to come in my marriage to Yosef? Would he be kind and caring, willing to patiently explain things to his young wife? Or would he be one of those men who is aloof and distant and harsh? And what about our children—what kind of father would he be?"

"A very good one," murmured Yeshua.

"But that was all in the future for me as a girl in her fifteenth year. The point is—I was immersed in my thoughts, and even feeling a little sorry for myself.

"And now to what Yosef wanted me to tell you."

Miriam paused to take a deep breath and reached for Yeshua's hand. She searched his face and then her gaze dropped as she continued.

"I was startled by a soft voice calling to me, 'Miriam.'

"It was a calm and very pleasant voice. A man dressed in a white cloak was standing on the garden path next to me. The whiteness of his garment surpassed anything I had ever seen.

"He smiled at me as I looked up at him. He said, 'Do not be afraid. I am Gabriel, a messenger of the Lord.'"

"Wait, wait, wait!" Yeshua interrupted her. "But this is much like the story Yohannon's mother told him! Gabriel, appearing to Zechariah!"

"As I later learned from her, yes."

"You speak so calmly, mother. Weren't you frightened?"

"No. There was such a great sense of calm and peace about him."

"This is astonishing! Was it a vision you were having?"

"No. The garden was quite real. The scent of the flowers was heavy in the air, and the bees were buzzing about. And the man standing by me had the loveliest, tender smile as he looked at me."

"What then?"

"He told me—" She took a deep breath and looked at her son. "He told me that I was chosen by the Lord to bear a special child but nothing would happen without my assent. And then he waited. I replied, 'I must tell Yosef this good news!' He was silent.

"'Yosef will be the father?' I asked him. It all sounded strange to me, coming immediately after my thoughts of what the future might hold.

"'No,' he replied.

"I said something like, 'Thank you for this offer but I am betrothed to Yosef and am a virgin.'

"He smiled. 'Yosef indeed will be your husband and a good father to your son and to the other children you will bear. But that is in your future.'

"My breath was taken away by what I was hearing. The man's eyes turned serious and he said, 'Miriam, you are needed for this task by the Lord. It is a new beginning. It will not take place without *you*.'"

Yeshua let out his own breath. "And you said yes."

"I did. Yes."

"And then?"

"Then Gabriel smiled with a joyous smile and he reached out both hands and placed them on my head. He spoke in a tongue I do not know, and as he spoke I felt warmth within my midsection that grew and grew until I felt as though my whole body was glowing. He then spoke in our own tongue, wonderful words I scarcely can remember, a long praise hymn to the Lord, honoring me for all that would come about through this child I was to bear. It ended and he told me what you were to be named. And he told me of things to come.

"He finished and the warmth receded and I felt a sudden listlessness as though I were about to faint. I did not, but when I lifted my gaze he was gone."

She looked at Yeshua. "That was the glorious day."

He stared at her intently. "This was about me. About my growing in your womb."

"Yes."

"This is not some childhood dream? It truly happened?"

"Yes. As I have said."

"You are telling me that Yosef is not, was not, my father?"

She nodded. "For some reason known only to the Lord, Yosef was not your birth father. But he was a true father to you."

"Yes," replied Yeshua.

She reached out a hand and touched his cheek. "He loved you with a father's deep love, Yeshua. And you *are* special. Not just to me but to many people. Ezra and Tobias have told everyone how you helped them to reconcile. Not only them. You are compassionate and kind and wise to so many people. You have grown strong and true in the Lord."

Yeshua shifted his gaze from her steady clear eyes. "When I am alone and the carpentry does not distract me, I have wondered about things. That time in Yerushalayim, for example. Other times, when everything seemed so clear for a moment or two. Brief images in my mind of places other than Nazareth. But this—this account of yours!"

He raised his eyes again to hers. "What about the future? What Gabriel told you?"

"In good time. I need to find my peace with it."

Yeshua let go of her hand. "I cannot believe the Lord acts in such a way. It sounds like one of the Greek stories we would laugh at in the rabbi's class. Zeus and the gods and what that lot could do. And Olympias, mother of Alexander the Great, claiming her son was the result of a lightning flash to her womb. Pagan stories!" He paused, thinking. "Were you familiar with such tales?"

"My father asked the same. No. Never. We were not taught such heathen tales."

"What did father say?"

Miriam laughed, "Which one? Mine or yours?"

"Mine."

"I was so very young! I thought, 'I have been honored by a messenger from the Lord! Me, Miriam of Cana! How wonderful! Now all of life will be joy and peace!' What followed was anything but joy and peace."

She glanced at her son. "I am tired with the remembering. People will be coming soon. It may be best for us to continue at a later time."

"Mother, now. I want to hear the rest."

She sighed. "Very well. This is the hard part."

Chapter 14

"It was my secret," Miriam continued. "I told no one. Mother was giving me instruction daily on how I was to do things in my new life. Days passed and I began to think it truly had been a beautiful daydream brought on by my fears of going to a strange new house. But then . . . ."

She broke off and touched his face.

"You are a grown man. Surely you must know about the rites women observe when they have their monthly blood. The special arrangements."

"I am aware of what my sisters observe."

"It was fairly new to me, but I had always been regular in my time of the month. Mine did not come. With a sinking feeling I counted carefully the days I was past due. I waited for another week. Nothing. My mother had noticed, and one afternoon she spoke to me directly about it. I did not know what to say—I was so young then. Question after question. I finally told her what I have just now told you."

"And?"

"She searched my face for a moment and then she laughed and told me I was a silly thing and I needed to eat more. She said she knew positively that I had not been with any man and what I said was impossible.

"This state of affairs went on for another week of no bleeding, at the end of which she took me to my father's study room and had me repeat what I had said to her.

"Father looked at me sternly. 'Tell me truly, have you been with a man in this way?'

"I said no. He looked at my mother. He asked her if there was any possibility I had been with a man. Mother said 'no', and she began to weep.

"'How can this be true,' she cried. 'We have always been faithful to the Lord. Why has this happened to upright people? Our child, our only child, whom we love! We must do something, but what?'

"My father told her to calm herself and said they needed to think things through.

"He turned to me and gave me a long look. 'Miriam, I love you deeply. Now answer me truly.' 'Yes, father, I always will,' said I. He went on. 'In recent weeks when other rabbis from our region came to study with me, were you listening? Did you hear us speak of the Daniel scroll held by the holy community of Qumran?' 'No father,' I replied, 'never.'"

Yeshua was puzzled. "Why did he ask that?"

"He told me later that the scroll of Daniel at Qumran mentioned a messenger of God by the name of Gabriel."

"The same name that the person in the garden gave you."

"Yes."

"And then?"

"Long faces around the house. He and my mother talked for quite a while, but the door to his study was closed firmly and I could hear nothing. The next day my father arranged a meeting with Yosef and his parents. Such an honorable man, my father!

"But Yosef was busy with matters in the shop. So it was several days before we met with them. And every morning before we went to Nazareth mother asked me if there was any change. There was no change. So off we three went to Nazareth at last.

"Yosef was finishing up a project. He had asked his parents to greet us and he would be along shortly. We were ushered into the dining room and took our seats around the table. After a few pleasantries, a long silence followed.

"My father, so honor bound to do the right thing, broke the silence by asking if Yosef would be along soon. Yosef's mother said it was quite agreeable to him for us to go ahead and speak of whatever we wished to see them about."

Mariam sighed. "So. After a few minutes of waiting, father asked me to give my account once more in front of Yosef's parents. I was frightened, but I did. Throughout my brief recital, Yosef's father nodded pleasantly at me but the face of Yosef's mother grew harder and harder. When I finished, there was a long cold silence.

"At last, Yosef's father cleared his throat several times and said, 'Well.'

"Father had kept his eyes on him throughout my account and now said, 'My wife and I believe our daughter. I realize it is a difficult tale to comprehend. I ask you to do so.'

"Silence. Father and mother joined hands. At last, father nodded and spoke softly.

"'It may be too difficult for you. You are entitled to break the betrothal covenant if you wish.'

"Yosef's father beamed at me and said, 'She certainly is a lovely child. Imagine! A messenger from the Lord!'

"Yosef's mother gave a loud sniff and leaned forward. She studied me. 'A young, pretty face goes best with such a pious story. But I want my son to know of the matter before any more is said. I will go fetch him from his work and tell him of our conversation before we return.'

"She rose and left the room.

"It was perfectly clear to everyone but Yosef's father what was about to happen. The betrothal would end. My family would be disgraced forever and probably have to move to another town. I would be tainted goods and never marry.

"The wait seemed to go on forever. From somewhere on the other side of the house, we heard voices, muffled by the distance, the mother's voice angry and high pitched. Occasionally it was interrupted by Yosef's lower tone. The voices stopped and there were footsteps. Yosef's mother swished through the doorway curtain. She sat with a thump in her chair and crossed her arms over her chest.

"'He is thinking of what to say.' She smiled at me, a wintry smile.

"More waiting. The air grew heavy in the room. I began to feel quite faint. My mother began to weep.

"The doorway curtain was pushed aside and Yosef entered. He looked only at me with a direct gaze. I returned it without flinching. At last he spoke.

"'Miriam, this account that my mother reports to me is a strange one indeed. You are young and as yet not acquainted with the ways of the world.'

"He paused. Our eyes remained locked. I kept silent.

"'Do you swear by the Lord that you have spoken truly?'

"'Yes.'

"'You swear by the Lord that you have been with no man?'

"'I do. No man.'

"He glanced at his parents. His father smiled genially at me. His mother spoke, hissing the words like sharp knives. 'An inspection will show the truth of this sorry tale.'

"Yosef raised a hand to silence her. She gave a snort of disapproval and settled in her chair.

"Yosef looked again at me. 'When my mother told me just now of your words, anger rose up in me at your treachery. I could not bear to face you again, such was my rage.'

"He paused and then went on. 'But I told my mother I would come here to see your parents and you face to face. As I crossed to this room, my anger cooled. You are young. I do not wish your life to be ruined. I thought the answer is to end the betrothal quietly and we go our separate ways in Nazareth and Cana. Such things are rare but not unheard of.'

"Yosef looked at me and his eyes softened. 'But you have sworn by the Lord. You are a rabbi's daughter and you know what that means.' He ran a hand through his hair.

"'I cannot believe the Lord acts in the way you describe.' Another snort came from his mother. 'Yet you have told my parents and now me that the Lord has done just that.'

"He paused and his mother murmured an epithet. He raised his eyebrows as he looked at her. When she said nothing, his gaze returned to me.

"'Yes,' I affirmed.

"His gaze turned harder, more intense. The room was very still except for my mother's steady weeping. Yosef spoke at last.

"'I cannot comprehend what has happened. It is a test of faith.'

"'Yes.' I said.

"'It seems I must trust you,' he replied.

"His eyes were on mine for another long moment. At last he nodded. 'Very well.'

"He looked at his parents and mine. 'I do not wish the betrothal covenant to be broken. I will honor it and pay the bride-price myself.'

"Mother's weeping ended with a choked sob. She reached over and took my hand. Father let out a long sigh of withheld breath.

"Yosef's mother hugged herself more tightly. Her son said to her, 'There will be no gossip. Mother, this is my command. Do you understand?'

"She muttered, 'As you wish, my son.'

"Yosef's father gave me a huge smile and slapped his hands on the table. 'Good!' he said. 'Now that that's settled, I'm off to the garden again.' He stood. 'Imagine! A messenger from the Lord!'"

Miriam's voice ceased. Yeshua realized with a start that her hand had been tightly holding his for some time. She released his hand and looked about. Women were approaching from the side streets.

"Others are coming," she said briskly. "We had best fill our jugs." She turned to him and smiled. "I have long pondered these things in my heart. I will tell you more, but not now."

Chapter 15

They had just begun their homeward journey from the well when Elisheva rushed to meet them. "Please hurry," she cried and then had to pause to catch her breath.

"What is it, child?" Miriam asked quickly, for Elisheva was not one who often hurried.

"Shimeon," and the daughter gasped for more air before continuing. "He went to the field of Leoti . . . to earn money . . . for throwing stones at the ravens . . . that eat the barley. But come, come quickly."

She turned and together they moved rapidly along the street. Elisheva gave them more details between breaths. "He ate the bread and vegetables that you had prepared for him. He was telling of his victories in the field. Suddenly he slumped over."

"What is it? Can you tell?" Miriam anxiously questioned.

"A sudden high fever. He is unconscious."

"Oh, dear," murmured Miriam. Her steps quickened.

"Yaakob and Yosa have carried him to his bed. And for once Yehudah is speechless."

They reached the house and entered. Without removing her headscarf or shawl, Miriam hurried through to the room her fifteen-year-old son shared with Yosa and Yehudah. Yeshua lowered the jugs of water to the kitchen hearth and followed her.

Shimeon lay on his pallet on the floor, his eyes closed. Yohannon and Rebekah stood by the door of the room, peering in. Yaakob rose as they entered. He held an earthen bowl filled with water in one hand and a damp cloth in the other.

"I have been applying cool water to try to calm the fever," he told them.

Miriam knelt by her son and felt his forehead and his neck. Yaakob and Yeshua exchanged glances.

"Too much warm sun in the field with ravens?" Yeshua asked quietly.

"Perhaps," his brother replied. "But he took his broad hat with him and was wearing it when he came home."

"This is more than sun fever," their mother said. "Help me to get his tunic off."

They bent and helped her pull the tunic up and over Shimeon's head until only his loincloth remained on his thin body. Miriam placed her palm on his stomach, and then on each of his legs in turn.

"High fever all over," she noted and rose. "Keep applying the wet cloth, especially to his abdomen. He may have eaten a poison weed in the field without thinking." She beckoned to Yeshua. "Come help me pour out the new water." She spoke to Rebekah, who stood just outside the doorway. "Do you remember the herbs we used with the neighbor's fever last winter?"

A nod from her daughter. "Good. They are in the red bowl in the pantry. Press them with a little water and make a fine paste." Rebekah left.

She spoke to the others. "If he ate something that upsets his stomach, the paste dissolved in water will help it pass quickly."

They left the room as Yaakob continued to wet the cloth in the water bowl and apply it to his unconscious brother.

The fever persisted into the early morning hours. Yeshua was now alone at his brother's bedside. The boy's breathing grew shallower.

The light from the olive oil lamp cast a narrow pool of light around the two brothers, one still and the other bending and bending again with the remoistened cloth. A memory came to him of the day when his father had confronted those whose boys had taunted Shimeon on his way home from school.

The recollection stirred another. The words of a prayer his father spoke on several occasions at the side of a sickbed of members of the synagogue. Once a wife had asked the source of such a wonderful prayer. Yosef responded simply, "It came to me in a dream." But this was no dream and his brother was very ill with a strange malady. And so Yeshua prayed.

"Our Heavenly Father, look upon our sins with mercy. Forgive us, Lord, for all our presumption and waywardness. Trusting in your forgiveness, I humbly come before you and ask that you will restore to health Shimeon, whom we love. I ask this in your Most Holy Name, for yours is the kingdom, the power, and the glory. Amen."

He continued with his ministrations through the long night. Before dawn he lay on the floor, exhausted, and slept beside his brother.

He woke to find his mother kneeling by Shimeon. Still groggy from sleep, Yeshua pushed himself to a sitting position by the wall. "How is he?"

Miriam turned to him with a radiant smile. "The fever has broken, thanks be to the Lord." Her smile turned to a look of concern. "Yeshua, you look exhausted. Go lie down in your own room and sleep. We can take care of him now."

He had no argument with that idea and made his way to his bed and fell back to sleep almost immediately.

Time

The sound of loud voices awoke him. He rose and found the source in the dining room. He saw the remains of the midday meal and, to one side, Shimeon. The faces and voices of his family reflected amazement and joy. Rebekah looked at Yeshua and spoke clearly above the clamor.

"Shimeon, show Yeshua this miracle of yours!"

Shimeon turned, beaming. "Look, brother!" Step by step he made his way towards Yeshua. In ten short steps there was no sign of a limp. Both legs walked strong and true.

Amid the hubbub of voices behind him at the table, Shimeon looked up at Yeshua and exclaimed, "No one will make fun of me now!"

But Yeshua was watching his mother, who was giving him a long look of speculation.

Chapter 16

In the days that followed Shimeon's recovery, Miriam parried Yeshua's requests to meet again privately and speak further about what she had told him at the well. "Not now," she would say.

In truth, she had much more than usual to oversee. The very day of the meal at which Shimeon walked freely, she held a family council to discuss the matter. We thank the Lord, Miriam said, but she added that she did not want their home besieged by the ill and the lame in Nazareth and surrounding villages, all clamoring to be healed. She expressed her viewpoint that the healing should be kept from neighbors and other townspeople for a short time. During those days she would introduce the subject of his illness and gradual recovery in daily conversations at the well. In later days she would convey her amazement that the Lord had favored her son not only with a return to good health but also the recovery of the use of his left leg. Strange the way that fevers worked, she would note, so that illness sometimes brought great healing. In time, with a united front by the whole family, the matter would become commonplace knowledge and Shimeon could appear in public again.

Hearing her plan, Shimeon groaned. "Does this mean I must stay in the house?" Miriam tousled his hair. "For a short while." She smiled. "It also means no more stoning of ravens in the field. I promise," a look at the three older sons, "that a more important task will be found for you by Yeshua, Yaakob, and Yosa." It was their turn to groan.

That same evening news came of a tragedy at the quarry outside Nazareth. The son of Mishael the stonemason had been killed in an accident. There were funeral arrangements to be made and the rites observed before the routine of daily life resumed. Shimeon, however, was to remain at home.

On one of Shimeon's "at home days," he was in the carpentry workroom with his three brothers, stacking new wheat sifters for the area's next wheat harvest when Miriam tapped at the door and entered. She seemed nervous.

"Hephaestion of Cana is here to see you, Yeshua. He did not say what the purpose of his visit is. I hope it is not dissatisfaction with the furniture we sold him."

Yeshua stopped hammering metal studs into the bottom side of a threshing sledge. He laid it on the worktable. "It's been much too long since then," he said mildly. He wiped his hands on his work apron and hung it on a hook.

He followed his mother to the entryway at the front of the house. A heavyset older man wearing a sumptuous cloak and a worried countenance awaited them, impatiently tapping the fingers of one hand against the doorjamb.

"My son, as you requested, Sir." Miriam announced and curtsied.

"Thank you, mother," her son said, smiling. "Hephaestion and I will talk in the garden."

They walked out and around to the gate and into the garden. Yeshua gestured the visitor to a seat on the bench and then sat himself.

"How may I help you?" he asked.

"Help is precisely what I need!" Hephaestion exclaimed. He eyed Yeshua with a measuring glance. Evidently satisfied with what he saw, he continued.

"We have not met, but the man in charge of my household remembers you well from two autumns ago, when you brought the furniture to us. He and others I have questioned give a good report of you." He stroked his cloak. "And your mother is a daughter of the former rabbi at Cana some years ago."

"I hope the furniture has been satisfactory," murmured Yeshua.

"Oh, certainly, certainly. Excellent quality." The visitor became agitated, clasping and unclasping his hands.

"What help do you wish?"

"It is a tale of great sadness, followed by joy, and now, now I am in the period of sadness again."

"The tale begins?"

"Yes, yes, the start of it all." He smoothed the front of his cloak. "I am Hephaestion of Cana. The name is an illustrious and uncommon one. Long ago an ancestor served with Alexander's general of the same name and later took it as his own when he married and settled in Galilea. Long ago.

"But now to my own story. As you will remember, I live north of Cana in a sizable house with commensurate staff to take care of all the matters that a substantial property requires." He paused.

Yeshua nodded. "Your many olive and fig trees are well tended, the orchard of apple trees is large, and the fields are maintained in good condition."

"Ah, you have an observing eye. Yes, I hire good laborers and the estate is well kept, but that's part of the problem, you see. If I were a poor man, living simply, none of this would have happened." The landowner turned to face Yeshua. "It all began when my wife died. She was so good with our younger son. The older one takes after me."

"You speak of a family matter and sigh," said Yeshua. "You are a man of faith. Why have you not spoken to your rabbi in Cana?"

"That's just it." Hephaestion gazed at the garden. "I fear to do so."

"I understand he is a godly man."

"Oh certainly, certainly. No doubt of that. A holy man."

He turned pleading eyes to Yeshua. "The rabbi is young. Not yet attuned to the ways of large landowners. And his wife is clearly the master in the household. Poor man. Furthermore, the fool confides in her and then word of even the most confidential matters quickly gets out in Cana and beyond. But I have heard that you are both wise and discreet. As your father was before you, blessed be his joy in the everlasting arms of the Lord."

He stopped and looked down at the ground and up again at Yeshua. "Please help me."

"I will if I can. Please continue with your story."

"Very well. I have two sons, one in his twenty-eighth year and the other in his twenty-third. Neither has married as yet. All was well until my wife died several years ago. The older son grieved for the time of mourning and prayers. Then he went on with his work. But my younger one, well, I don't know how to describe it."

"He held his grief close."

"Exactly. I tried to speak with him and comfort him, but he turned away. The worst of it was, he began to sulk. So undignified for a young man of his standing! At last, one day he came to me. 'Father,' he said, quite firmly, 'I am not meant for country life. I wish to see the wider world. Travel to Yerushalayim, Alexandria, perhaps even Rome.'

"We had quite a long conversation. He persuaded me of his plan, and the Lord knows my son had been of little use since his mother died. I offered him a set allowance, to be paid periodically, but he said 'absolutely not.'

"I was stunned by what followed. He demanded, *de-manded,* his share of the estate. Not at my death. Not once he assumed proper responsibility of his share of work. Not upon marriage, with children to follow. Oh no, he demanded it *now*."

"I have never heard of such a thing," Yeshua murmured.

"Nor have I! I was tempted to whip him for his insolence and haughty manner."

"Did you?"

"No. I was so aghast at what he suggested, and by the manner in which he spoke to me, that I told him in very firm tones, I assure you, that I needed time to think upon what was said. The conversation ended with him stomping angrily out of the room."

"He has been sulking around the house ever since?"

"No, no, this was a year ago, last winter. Your furniture delivery preceded these events in the autumn."

"An old story."

"Yes, yes, but I tell you the beginning of it to understand the horror that followed. For seven days we did not meet. During that time thoughts of my late wife all but consumed me. She was a beautiful woman and a good wife. My own grief at her passing was great. She cared for our oldest, but it was the young one who claimed her deepest love. These memories haunted me. On the eighth day I summoned my son and told him coldly that I would do as he wished. His share came to one-third, with a share of the remainder to serve as my sustenance in my old age, and the final third to go to my elder son. The young pup asked how soon he might receive his share. I restrained my anger and told him three fields or more needed to be sold as his share. As soon as the sale was completed, he would have his money."

"How did your older son take these arrangements?"

"That very day I told him. He called me 'old fool' and refused his own share until the proper time. The language with which he described his brother was shocking. In fact his angry behavior was no better than his brother's arrogance." Hephaestion hung his head. "And *he* stomped out of the room."

"The money was raised?"

"Oh, yes. Not easily. It required using receipts from a quarter of the harvest the previous spring in addition to the sale of the fields. The timing was terrible and I sold at quite a loss. But the money was raised and paid out. A large sum."

He turned to Yeshua. "You can understand why I did not go to the rabbi. I had no desire to be the laughingstock of the Cana countryside."

"I sense there is even more of this sorry tale."

"Oh, yes. Yes, indeed. All was quiet for a while, and then my older son informed me that his brother had gone no farther than Caesarea, on the coast, where he was spending his fortune on loose women at the drinking houses outside the wall of the city."

"You believed the stories?"

"Of course not. I knew of the vengeful nature of my older son and his scorn for me. But the stories kept coming, so this past winter I swore my farm manager to secrecy and sent him to Caesarea to establish the truth of the matter."

He looked at Yeshua. "The truth was even more terrible. In an incredibly short time, the huge sum my son received was gone. Wasted. Squandered. Not in any of the places he had cited to me in his request for his inheritance—Yerushalayim, Alexandria, even Rome. Oh, no! He was drunk in Pilate's nearby city. The shame of it all! My farm manager relieved my anxieties on one score. He reported that the family name had never been relied upon for credit. Probably my son was in a drunken stupor and had forgotten his own name."

"How terrible!" Yeshua exclaimed.

"Oh, but there is more! His money gone, the party was over and his degradation was complete, for he now relied upon the good will of a retired centurion who had given him work feeding swill to the swine on his farm."

"Unbelievable!" Yeshua sucked in his breath.

"Yes, but there is even more! His housing was in a tumbledown hut on the swine field, and my man told me that he definitely saw my son eating the carob pods he was feeding the swine."

"From worse to worse."

"Yes. My man told me—he did not want to tell me but I pressed him—of his fear that my son would not live much longer under these conditions."

"Did you go after him?"

"And incur even greater scorn from my older son, who daily passed by me with an 'I told you so' under his breath? He thought I could not hear him, but I heard him, oh yes, I heard him."

"Such a terrible time you have had. There is more?"

"When my rage subsided, I lost all interest in life and possessions. I retired to the flat rooftop. I ordered that only a small table, chairs, and cushions were to be brought up, along with a sleeping pallet. The weather was warmer, but when it rained it rained on me; when the sun shone, it shone on me. I became a recluse, with my meals sent up from below."

Hephaestion paused and his eyes filled with tears. "I am grateful to the Lord that he remained with me through this mad spell. As time passed I began to pray. For I prayed, oh, how I prayed. Then one day," Hephaestion paused to wipe away his tears.

"Please, take your time," murmured Yeshua.

"No, no. This is the good part. One afternoon I was sitting in my chair on the roof. Far, far down the road I saw something moving; it seemed no larger than a sheep. It drew closer, closer, until I could see it was the figure of a man. Closer still, and I could tell it was a tramp, dressed in the poorest of clothes. As the poor fellow drew nearer, I suddenly realized it was my son!

"Weary as I was from the days and nights on the roof, I leapt from my chair, took the stairs two at a time and ran forth to meet my son. All I could think was, 'My son, my lost son is coming home.'"

For the first time, Hephaestion smiled.

"I reached him. My old legs had more energy than his. And what a sight he was! Shrunken, dull eyes, a face that was gray and haggard. His hair was uncut, as was his beard, and his cloak was soiled and torn.

"'Father, forgive me,' he started to say, but I was so glad to see him! I kept hugging and kissing him, my son who was lost but now had returned! Tears of joy streamed from my eyes as I put an arm around his shoulders and helped him walk to the home he had abandoned. He bathed and rested. I woke him. We had a celebration feast that night!"

The mood of Hephaestion darkened. "But his brother would not come. I sent several messengers to the field where he was working. He told them in no uncertain terms that he would not come. At last I rose from the feast table and went to the field where he was supervising the workers.

"He shouted at me. At me, his father! In front of the other men in the field! 'Old man,' he raged, 'my brother is dead to me!'"

Hephaestion's eyes had filled with tears once more. He turned to Yeshua. "And that is where matters stand. I hear you are a wise man. Please help me untangle this awful mess!"

Yeshua thought for a long moment as the other man wiped his eyes. "Your older son. You have guaranteed his share to him?"

"Yes. I have gone further. I have told him that he is just as dear to me as his brother, but he will not listen. I have said that he is with me always, but his brother had to learn a very hard lesson away from home. He scoffs. I even have told him that we are much alike and that his cold rage will consume him as once happened to me before I met his mother. He will not listen. Now my heart is broken again."

Yeshua looked directly at him. "And he may not be able to hear you for some time." He thought for a moment. "They have both disobeyed you, their father. The younger seems to have learned his lesson. May the Lord see that it sticks! The older brother, well, he has shown you disrespect and scorned you. He has forgiven neither his brother nor you."

"I see that. What can I do to restore harmony?"

"Your younger son, what will he live on now that his share is spent?"

"I will give him work in the field and pay him a wage. As my son he will live in the house. At my death, he will inherit half of my share."

"He knows this?"

"I will tell him when he is more rested. I have assured him about the work. It eased his mind. No more carob pods in a pig pen."

Yeshua sighed. "It is difficult. Your older son is disheartened by the celebration of the return. In time he may come to believe in your good will and steadfastness toward him. But not yet. The problem is forgiveness. You have forgiven your son, but he needs to seek it also from his brother. And his brother must ask forgiveness from you for his hardhearted behavior."

Yeshua frowned. "The difficulty is that forgiveness is only forgiveness when it is freely given, as was yours toward your son. You, the father, cannot impose forgiveness on either son."

Hephaestion nodded. "You see why I need your help."

Yeshua spoke gravely. "There is no easy solution. It will take time. You must assure your sons that you love them both. In time, if they mature and grow wiser, they will reconcile. Your meals together are important. There may be long silences. Your own even-handed steadiness is the key."

"I fear my years remaining are few, Yeshua."

Yeshua was silent for a moment, peering at the older man. At last he smiled and spoke.

"You will have sufficient years and more for the worthy task set before you. Do not grow weary before it is accomplished. I will pray to our Father in heaven to give you patience, and you must continue daily in your own prayers lest you fall into a terrible rage again."

Hephaestion considered what Yeshua had said. He nodded and stood.

"Thank you. May I come again?"

Yeshua rose. "You are always welcome."

They clasped hands. Tears again filled the eyes of Hephaestion. "Thank you, Yeshua of Nazareth," he said softly, and turned toward the gate and was gone.

CHAPTER 17

EARLY THAT EVENING YESHUA and Miriam sat at one end of the dining table. Yaakob and Yosa had returned to the workshop, and the others were busy with evening chores. Miriam was counting out the week's receipts from two large leather pouches. Yeshua had hoped that she would tell him more of her strange tale once they were alone. It was clear that she did not want her other children to hear their conversation.

"The spring harvest has been one of the best!" she exclaimed as she finished her counting. "It is almost time for the shearing of the flock, and the sale of milk from our cow continues to bring in more than enough for her keep." She glanced at Yeshua. "Please commend Rebekah on her work. She is more thorough in the stable than Elisheva ever was and she makes no fuss."

"I will, mother."

"The sifters and sledges have sold well, and the six carts sold mark a growing demand."

"Indeed," her son replied. "We are almost out of the different woods. Yaakob knows a man who will give us a good price. What do you count?"

"More than enough to replenish the wood." She began to scoop up the coins. "Forty Tyrian shekels and twice as many silver dinars. A very good harvest, indeed. And you have a dozen new plows ready for the time of planting."

Her sleeve brushed a stack of dinars; one fell to the floor and rolled across the room. It wobbled once, twice, and fell through a crack in the wooden floor.

Miriam rose from the table. "I keep telling you and your brother to fix that crack!"

"It is only a dinar, mother."

"You do not go to the market. Prices are up recently."

Yeshua had joined her. They stood gazing down at the crack.

"I will tear out the one board and replace it," he said.

"No, no. This has happened before. I have a method for rescuing lost coins."

She walked into the adjoining kitchen and returned with two hardened reeds from a reed box beside the hearth. Kneeling on the floor, she carefully inserted the two reeds through the crack.

She grunted. "More light is needed. Bring the lamp from the table."

Yeshua brought the oil lamp and knelt beside her.

"Good, good," she murmured and probed with the reeds. "Got it," she exclaimed and pulled the dinar up between the two reeds through the crack. "The lost is recovered!"

They returned to the table with the lamp. "But you really do need to fix that crack," she advised. Her eyes softened as she looked at his face more closely in the light of the lamp.

"You have been working too hard. Let Yaakob and Yosa carry more of the burden."

"They do their full share."

"Well, let them do more." Miriam poured the large coins into one pouch and the smaller sizes into the other. "You are widely respected and knowledgeable about the furniture and farm implements made here. It would be wise to take Yosa along on one of your trips. He can handle the farmers. He has a pleasing manner and is at ease in farm life conversation."

"It is not the work. I have not slept well for several nights and, truth is, the dreams are strange."

"Yes?"

"No, no. These things are not for a woman's ears."

Miriam frowned and responded airily, "Oh, well, I am only—"

With a laugh Yeshua interrupted her, "Yes, yes, you are only my mother, whose favorite sayings are written forever on my heart." He smiled. "Let us speak instead of your betrothal and the outcome. You and father *did* marry. And I *was* born."

"Your father had dreams. He was a very practical man who lived by the work of his hands. But he had dreams."

"Yes. Even at the last. "

"Tell me about *your* dreams." She gave him a long look.

"You first," Yeshua prompted.

"After you."

"Very well," Yeshua sighed. "In one I was alone in a cave on a barren hillside." He paused.

"More."

"Promise to tell me of father's dreams?"

"I'm next."

He smiled. "I have seen you bargain in the marketplace. And learned from you."

"Flattery will not work. More."

"Very well. In the dream I was sitting at the mouth of a cave, behind a hollowed out place in which rainwater had collected. To one side of the rain basin there was a small carob tree with many ripe pods dangling from its branches.

"It was very hot even though I was shielded from the sun by the upper lip of the cave. I looked to the horizon but there was no sign of any habitation. No sign of vegetation other than the carob tree near me.

"Time passed. I slept upright.

"As I sat sleeping, I began to dream within the dream. I opened my eyes and spied a motion. Looking down the hillside I saw a dust devil, a small whirlwind turning on a level place with the sun glinting off it. It whirled but did not move from its position.

"From within the whirlwind I heard a voice. It was an ingratiating and wheedling voice like one heard in the market from farmers whose produce is not fresh."

"What did the voice say?" Miriam asked.

"That I need not be suffering in the desert. That I was made for far more important things. I saw images form and reform within the whirlwind, images showing me the wonders that I could work, the holiness and fame I could have, the power that could be mine to wield over an empire far greater than that of Alexander or Caesar Augustus.

"The sly, whispering voice spoke, and with each image I felt as though my heart was pierced through and through. The pain was terrible, yet somehow I had the strength to counter the falsehoods, to reply in words of holy scripture to refute the tempting images and the seductive voice. Despite my physical weakness, again and again I replied, and, as I did, I felt myself growing stronger.

"The dream within the dream ended at last.

"Again I sat at the mouth of a desert cave, behind a hollowed out place in which rain water had collected. To one side of the rain basin there was a small carob tree, now with fewer ripe pods dangling from its branches.

"My eyelids were heavy from lack of sleep. I leaned against the wall of the cave and slept. I awoke to the sound of a great thunderstorm. The wind cooled me as rain fell upon the landscape.

"I struggled to stand and stripped off my cloak and danced naked in the downpour, my mouth uplifted to catch the fresh water. But I was so very weary I could not dance for long. I shuffled back into the cave and fell asleep against the nearest wall. It was a long, long sleep.

"In the dream I wakened once more. My awakening came with a marvelous view. As far as I could see, the desert floor was alive with flowers and herbs and plants that could be eaten. What a wonderful sight! I laughed for joy!

"And then I awoke once more, truly awoke, to the sound of Yaakob snoring. It all was only a dream."

He raised his eyes to meet his mother's even gaze.

"You were not frightened?" Miriam asked softly.

"No."

"Your study of scripture all these years has been worthwhile—if only for dreams."

They were silent for a time, mother and son, contemplating the dream and what it might mean.

He reached a hand out and touched her. "Now tell me one of father's dreams. I need relief from the vivid memory of my own." He smiled. "But I am sure the carob tree in my dream came from part of the story told me by Hephaestion when he visited. And the thunderstorm was surely prompted by my brother's snores."

"You must not make light of these things," Miriam scolded. "Your father once had a dream that saved our lives, though other lives were lost."

"Tell me."

"It is too terrible."

"You promised."

She sighed a deep sigh. "It is not good to speak of old horrors. Yosef said we must have faith. Sometimes faith is a heavy burden."

"Tell me. It was his last wish."

Miriam withdrew from his touch. It was her turn to stare down at the table.

"It was a dream of blood."

"How so?"

Miriam looked up. "We remained in Bethlehem for some months after you were born." She grimaced. "Yours was not an easy birth, and my healing took time. So we stayed on. Yosef found us inexpensive lodging and sent a message to my uncle Cleopas to keep an eye on Yosef's parents and the house." She looked around. "Our house was simpler then, with fewer rooms. Not difficult to care for. And Cleopas knew a man from another village who could step in to see that some of the work was done.

"As for Yosef, he found work in Bethlehem. We survived, although they were hard times.

"One day magnificently clothed strangers arrived from the East. They oohed and aahed over you and told us we truly were blessed to have a son who was meant for great things. Yosef spoke to them. I was preoccupied with my own problems.

"After they left, Yosef came to me in great excitement. They had given expensive gifts, far more than even five years' profits from the Nazareth shop.

"'Now you can have the very best care,' he proclaimed. But that night he dreamed a terrible dream that was to change our lives dramatically. A dream of blood."

"Yours?"

"If you mean as a woman, no. I was much improved by then. It was a dream of other women, mothers crying over the bloody bodies of their young children. Soldiers were walking the streets of Bethlehem, knocking on doors and pulling infants and toddlers out, butchering them."

"Terrible!" exclaimed Yeshua.

"Yes. Yosef woke me before the first cockcrow and whispered these things in my ear. A horrible dream. I tried to calm him, but at the end of the telling, he rose from the bed and declared, 'We must go. Today. *Now*.'

"How awful."

"I was only half awake. You were by my side, mewing. I put you to my breast and struggled to a sitting position. 'It is a dream,' I cried. 'Why must we go?'

"He made no reply. Immediately he began packing our few belongings. In a short while he came to the door of the house with our donkey and loaded me and you and two sacks with our belongings on it. And so we went. To Egypt, the land where long ago another Yosef rose to sit at the right hand of Pharaoh."

"So sudden," Yeshua murmured.

"Uprooted like that, yes. But for a reason. As we traveled we heard along the way stories of how King Herod had received the men from the East. He had inquired of his palace priests where they might go and they told him, Bethlehem."

Yeshua sighed. "Poor judgment by the men from the East. Asking for help from Herod! The soldiers in father's dream—Herod's soldiers?"

"Yes. It was in the last year of Herod's reign." Miriam gave her son a sad smile. "Lost in his fears of conspiracies on all sides. Some said he had gone mad. Many of his own wives and children—poisoned or executed. And those children in Bethlehem—two years of age or younger. He had to root out the threat from a future rival."

Yeshua nodded. "I have heard stories but I had not heard of this trip to Egypt until you mentioned it the other day. It was a wonderful thing, your escape. Paid for by men from the East."

"A dream," said Miriam. "That's what Yosef had. Through a sign from the Lord, we were spared. But not the others. Thirty or more infants and young children torn from their mothers' arms and savagely murdered." She looked at Yeshua. "But not you."

Miriam was lost in the remembering for a moment. She cleared her throat and continued.

"When news reached us of Herod's death, we rejoiced and soon after began the trip home to Nazareth. And here we have prospered since those terrible days."

Miriam tied the cords at the top of each coin pouch. "Enough of dreams," she said softly. "You were spared for a reason. But those children—they were all special to their mothers, too. I sometimes wonder what the meaning of it is. So long ago."

"Yes," agreed Yeshua.

She turned to him, her eyes like deep pools, and placed a hand on his. "Son, don't leave me."

Startled by the sudden change in conversation, Yeshua exclaimed, "Mother, how can you have such a thought!"

"My cousin's son coming. Yohannon. Asking you to join him. His first disciple to prepare the way for the Messiah."

Yeshua shook his head. "It was clear to me that he was mistaken. He will find other disciples."

"Perhaps. But there may be another meaning."

She withdrew her hand from his and rose from the table with a sigh.

"We must live in the days we have," she said. "Every one of them that you are here is a blessing from the Lord."

CHAPTER 18

Two DAYS LATER YEHUDAH was with the shepherds to help them move the family flock to spring pastures north of Nazareth. The four other brothers were in the carpentry workshop. Yaakob was showing Shimeon how to make the decorative incisions that added value to the panels that were to be used in furniture for a local official in Tiberias. Yeshua and Yosa looked on, remembering how their father Yosef had taught them this art in years past.

Yeshua smiled at the sight of Shimeon, no longer stoning ravens, so excited to be with his older brothers and learning new skills.

A tap at the door and Miriam entered, looking distressed.

"Yeshua, come over here." She pulled the door shut and leaned close to him. The others, engrossed in Yaakob's lesson, paid them no heed.

"The wife of Mishael the stonemason is here," she said in a low voice. "Leela is beside herself with worry about him. His grief over the tragedy of their son's death has sent him into madness. He sits in a dark room cursing, and he has barred the door so no one can bring him food or water. She fears for his life. You must speak to her."

Yeshua nodded and followed her to the dining room, where Mishael's wife sat tensely erect at the table. She leaped to her feet when she saw Yeshua coming and rushed to him and took his hand.

"You must speak to him! He will not speak to me or see the rabbi or the elders of the synagogue. You were childhood friends and he respects you and regards you as a fellow craftsman."

"It is about your son Avner."

"Yes." She wiped her eyes.

"We observed all the burial rites. Were they not a consolation?"

"At first. But later the same day he fell into a dark mood and sat stone-faced at meals. Three mornings ago he retreated to his workroom and has barred the door so no one can enter. I pled with him through the door but he only laughed a terrible laugh and cursed the Lord and all of Nazareth."

"I will come at once."

The house of Mishael was two streets away. Miriam walked with them. As they walked quickly, the details of the recent tragedy were fresh in his mind. Mishael and Leela had one son, Avner, six years of age.

Mishael in past weeks had been at work on the construction of a new house at the edge of Nazareth. On the day of the tragedy Mishael and Avner had gone to the nearby quarry to load a cart with stones to be used in the construction.

Avner was enthralled with the quarry and stood behind the donkey cart as it was loaded. Finally Mishael was again seated at the front of the cart. He was impatient to leave and called to his son to hurry up and join him. His donkey, startled, suddenly pulled forward and the stones shifted. Mishael's son was still behind the cart. He could not dodge the heavy stones falling off the end of the cart and fell beneath them, his chest crushed.

Yeshua, Miriam and Leela reached the house and rounded the far corner to the workshop door. A cartload of stones stood in the stone yard next to the workshop. Yeshua knocked loudly.

"Go away!" Mishael bellowed from within. "I want nothing."

"Is there another entrance?" Yeshua asked in a low voice. Leela shook her head.

"Mishael," he called out, "it is your friend Yeshua."

"I have no friends. Go away!"

"We have been friends since childhood."

"Go away!"

"I am still your friend. I want to come in and sit with you."

Silence.

"Unbar the door. I want to come in and sit with you."

"Is this a trick?"

"It is not a trick. I want to come in and sit with you."

Silence. Yeshua turned to Leela and spoke softly. "Let me do this thing alone so he does not think it is a ruse."

"But I must see him."

"You shall." Yeshua gave his mother a nod, and Miriam took Leela's arm. "It may take some time," Yeshua murmured. "Have courage. Go in the house."

Tears filled her eyes. He took both her hands in his. "Go," he urged. Miriam turned Leela away from the door and slowly the two of them went. Yeshua turned back to the door.

"Mishael?"

A voice came from within, near the door. "I heard the voice of Leela. Is she with you?"

"I told her to go in the house. I am alone. I want to come in and sit with you."

"Ha! You will ruin your reputation in Nazareth. Holy Yeshua visiting a crazy man!"

"I will wait here until you open the door."

"Then you soon will grow tired. I have nothing more to say to anyone."

"Then let me in and we will share silence."

The sound of a sob came from the other side of the door. Yeshua knocked loudly on the door and raised his voice. "You know that you can trust me. I am your friend."

After a moment there was the sound of a wooden bar being lifted. A hoarse voice said, "Come in then."

Yeshua pushed the door open. Sunlight flooded into the room. Tools were placed neatly in racks along the wall. Mishael reached a large stone, as yet unshaped, in a far corner and sat. He raised a hand to shield his eyes.

"Come in if you're coming in and shut the door."

Yeshua swung the door closed. He had made the heavy door for Mishael's father ten years before. It had been his first major project.

The closing of the door left the room in near darkness. He could barely make out the figure of Mishael in the corner. The room stank of emptied bowels. The harsh heavy odor was close to overwhelming.

A bitter laugh came. "Welcome to Sheol."

"Is there a chair in here?" asked Yeshua.

Mishael replied, his voice dripping with sarcasm. "Don't you remember, my friend? You make chairs. I work with stones. But no longer."

"Then I will stand," said Yeshua.

A long silence followed, broken only by the sound of flies buzzing.

At last Mishael spoke. "You are a holy man. Even the rabbi comes to you with questions he cannot answer. Why have you come? The Lord has judged me despicable and wretched."

"I am going to come and sit next to you," replied Yeshua. He carefully made his way to Mishael, avoiding the place where the flies were buzzing.

"I only have the one stone here," Mishael said.

"Then I will sit on the dirt floor next to you." He edged forward and sat. "I do not judge you."

A harsh laugh that became a coughing fit came from the other man.

"That is," Mishael sputtered as the fit eased, "that is because you are a fool and still believe in the Lord. The ideas of the Romans have more appeal. No hidden gods for them. Out in the open in great temples where you can see and touch. Jupiter. Neptune. And Caesar Augustus is the Divine Son. Orderly. Visible. A perfect world, eh?"

Yeshua did not reply.

"The Law and the Prophets are a joke," said Mishael at last. "King David had a man murdered so he could possess Bathsheba—yet the Lord favored him. Solomon the blessed was their son. What a great son—pah! Married to all those wives. And many more who were willing to pleasure him. Murdering his sons and rivals to the throne. What does your Law have to say to that? Is that your notion of the Lord? Where is the justice in that?"

Yeshua said nothing.

"You say you are my friend, "Mishael exploded, "but you do not respond with yea or nay to what I believe."

"My heart is listening to your great hurt."

"Remember the story of Herod's slaughter of the innocent infants in Bethlehem? So much for our precious children, hey? Where was the Lord, guardian of the faithful then? I piss on the Lord!"

"You love Avner."

A roar. "This is *not* about my son."

"You love Avner and he is gone. In the blink of an eye."

"Yes! Like the wheat sliding under the harvest sledge! But the harvest is death. Where is the justice in that?"

"You love Avner."

Another roar. "Who are *you* to lecture me about my only child! You are one of how many children? Seven! What do you know of my loss?"

"I feel it in my heart." Yeshua calmly replied. "I cannot grasp your deep hurt. Your only son. But I am your friend. Tell me how it is with you."

A string of curses from Mishael. Then silence. The silence was broken at last by sobs.

"Tell me."

The sobs subsided. "It is judgment on me and my iniquity."

"Tell me."

"No. It is unspeakable and I have been judged and Avner was taken from me."

"I am not your judge."

"Oh, truly? We shall soon see, my friend with the calm voice. Not my judge? Ha! Let me tell you a lovely story. A story about a man who lived in a certain town in Galilea. He was a stonemason. A very skilled one, with a wife who was good and loyal and true.

"One day he was visited by a man who wished to arrange for a new house to be built. He and his wife were moving from a village into town and he wanted a house more suitable to his prosperity. The work began.

"The day came when the other man was away in Tiberias and his wife came in her husband's place to view the progress on their new house. She was so taken with the man laying the stones that she invited him to come with her to their old house in the country for the midday meal. And so he did. And he stayed the afternoon, enjoying her charms."

Mishael stopped.

"You are the man," Yeshua said quietly.

Yeshua shifted his position on the earthen floor and reached up to rest a hand on Mishael's shoulder.

Silence. At last Mishael began to sob, and his voice was barely coherent.

"The next week, with Avner, I went to the quarry for more stone. And he died. Retribution from the Lord for my sin."

"No."

"Yes. You of all people should know. Judgment. What I deserve."

There was silence for a moment. Then Yeshua spoke calmly.

"You have done a terrible thing against yourself and Leela and the husband of the other woman. She was wrong to tempt you and your response was wrong. But hear me. Avner's death was not due to the wrath of the Lord. It was a terribly unfortunate accident."

A sigh from Mishael. "I was impatient with my son."

Silence.

"I shouted for him to join me. My cry startled the donkey."

Yeshua said gravely. "You are still a beloved child of the Lord."

"Oh, come! Do not be ridiculous. You are humoring me!"

"No. I believe this with all my heart, and you are still my friend."

"Truly?"

"Truly. What you have done is done and will always be with you. You must make amends if possible, unless it involves further hurt to your wife and the husband. You will need to look the woman in the eye and tell her 'never again.'

And you must let Avner rest in the mercy and love of the Lord and cherish the memory of him."

Mishael uttered a raw expletive. "I cannot. Go away."

"You can. There is a higher power for both of us."

"The temptation is great and I am weak."

"Yes. But you will have courage and the Lord will strengthen you."

"I am not sure about that. How can I know?"

"Hold my hand." Yeshua dropped his hand from Mishael's shoulder. He extended his hand into the darkness and it was grasped.

"Heavenly Father," Yeshua said quietly, "fill my friend Mishael with the Spirit of your presence in this room so that he may know I have spoken truly that he is not alone. You are with him in the darkness. Amen."

There was silence but the hands of the two men remained joined.

At last Yeshua spoke again. "Find another stonemason to complete the work."

Mishael's voice was calmer now. "I know of such a man."

"Good." Yeshua rose. "Stand up and come with me into the sunlight."

"I would rather remain here."

"I understand. But you are not a wild beast. You are Mishael, a beloved child of the Lord. Come to the light."

Silence.

Mishael's hand tightened on Yeshua's.

"I am going to stand up now," Yeshua said softly, "and I want you to stand with me."

"Yes."

The two men rose. As they walked slowly to the door, Yeshua put his arm around Mishael.

"Three things you must do," Yeshua said in the darkness.

"Oh, now you will tell me of the Law!"

"My friend Mishael, you have created your own burden. Give it up to the Lord."

"What then must I do?"

"Give Leela your love completely. Clean this room thoroughly. And ask the rabbi to come and pronounce a blessing on it when you have finished."

Yeshua pulled the wooden door open wide, and side by side the two men walked into the sunlight.

Chapter 19

Several days later Yeshua rose before dawn to begin loading a large cart with furniture he was taking that day to a buyer in Kapharnaum. He was leading the pony out from the stable room to hitch it to the cart as Miriam came to say goodbye, a packet for his lunch in one hand. Her eyes sparkled.

"You were preparing for your journey so I have not told you of the good news from Leela last evening at the well."

He finished his task and turned to her, smiling. "Mother, please tell me before you explode."

"Mishael has returned to his old self! Leela says it is more like his new and better self! Honestly, son, she glowed like a young bride!"

Yeshua's smile grew broader. "They have had two nights together. If this attention from Mishael continues, they may be blessed with another child soon."

"That is what she is hoping for! Have a good trip." She turned and danced to the house door in her pleasure at the news from Mishael's wife.

As Yeshua swung himself up to the seat at the front of the cart, Miriam called out to him. "Are you going the shore road way?"

"Yes. It calms my spirit, riding by the lake."

"If possible, please stop in Magdala and express our sympathy to Miriam over the loss of her husband Hosea."

"I will." She waved as he urged the pony forward and soon they were on a steady pace along the road.

Yeshua's father had sold many household items of wood in Tiberias, the seat of Herod Antipas' reign. Yosef's work was noted for its quality, and each sale had expanded his list of potential buyers in Tiberias and along the west side of the lake. In the last year before his death he had begun to send Yeshua in his place, and the son was well received.

Today, however, he passed the western outskirts of the city, taking the road that angled northeast to the lakeshore and Kapharnaum. Before midmorning he had reached Magdala and pulled up at the home of Hosea and Miriam.

The house was built so that a large verandah at the back provided a panoramic view of the lake. The ability to see fishing boats coming near had been important to Hosea, who owned a stretch of shorefront just down from the house. After a night on the lake, fishermen docked their boats in the early morning and arranged the sale to him of what they had caught. It was a thriving business, and Yeshua's father had constructed many special carts for Hosea to transport the day's catch to the market places of Tiberias and the neighboring villages.

After the recent death of Hosea, his wife was in charge. She was no stranger to the business. For many years she had kept all the accounts and knew to the copper coin any outstanding payments that villagers owed.

Hosea and Miriam were both younger than Yeshua's father Yosef. Contrary to custom, they had treated each other as equals. They were not afraid to voice strong opinions, and several times Yeshua himself had witnessed the two of them, toe to toe, arguing over a price to be calculated for the sale of a cartful of fish. He also had witnessed the two of them, the carts dispatched, holding each other and laughing about the argument.

Now she was alone. He shared his mother's concern about how the widow was handling the loss.

She emerged from the house at the sound of the pony cart drawing up. She ran to greet him as he alighted.

"Yeshua, what a lovely surprise!"

"I am on my way to Kapharnaum. Mother expressly wanted me to stop by and greet you. We all were saddened to hear of your loss."

"I am grateful." She looked away. "I thought this was the kind of thing that happens to others. Not us." She looked back at him and her face had tightened. "He did not suffer. Simply slumped over as he was rising from bed one morning and that was it. He was gone." She wiped sudden tears away. "But I am doing well, you can tell your mother that."

"My heart goes out to you. You two were an example of how love can deepen in a marriage."

She laughed. "Oh, we had our ups and downs. I remember you viewing some of our arguments about pricing the catch."

"Yes." He looked at her and noticed the new lines on her face. "I miss him, too. He was an honest and loving man. You were good for each other."

'Yes, we were." She took his arm in hers. "Enough gloom. Come sit out on the verandah and tell me the gossip of Nazareth. The fish carts have gone to the markets, and my accounts can wait."

They caught each other up on all the news. He recounted the story of Shimeon's illness and miraculous recovery. She told him tales of the tight-knit fishing community and asked him to take time to call on one of her favorites, a man named Zebadya.

Miriam laughed at his encounter with Ezra and Tobias and how things had turned out well. "Fishermen are more philosophical," she commented. "Until they fish too close to each other and their nets get all in a tangle."

At one point she turned serious, although her eyes smiled. "But the big news is, I have a suitor! A man with whom Hosea had business dealings in Tiberias. He sent me a message that he had something important to tell me and asked when would it be convenient for him to call on me."

"So soon!"

"Yes, but I did not know the nature of his conversation until he arrived. I thought it must be about some debt or another we owed. Or, miracle of miracles, though it seldom happens, payment to settle accounts owed by him to us. At any rate, he wasted no time getting down to the purpose of his call. 'I have come to ask if you will be my wife.' Well, Yeshua, I almost fainted away! He continued. 'This may seem irregular to you, as so little time has elapsed since your dear husband passed on to his heavenly reward. But I have spoken to my rabbi, a very learned man, and he assures me that at older ages it is best to get on with life.'"

"I am stunned," said Yeshua.

"As I was also. But he went on and on about how he had watched me from afar after his own wife had died some years ago, and he had come to the conclusion that we would be a perfect match, should the possibility arise. The marriage would hold great benefits for me, since I would be more respectable because of his position and therefore able to circulate in Tiberias society."

"The audacity of the man!"

"Yeshua, the worst of it was that his demeanor was serious and sincere. I had to bite my lip to keep from breaking out in peals of laughter. Honestly, the thought of me mingling in 'respectable' society!"

"I hope you shortly sent him on his way."

"Soon enough. But first I thanked him for his coming and honoring me with a proposal of marriage. However, I told him, I am perfectly able to face life on my own. Besides, I have a thriving fish business to run.

"Well! At that last remark about 'business,' his face lighted up and he allowed as how he was in a position to manage it from Tiberias. He knew someone who would be excellent as an 'on the scene manager' here in Magdala. That did it for me! A few more polite comments on both sides and I showed him to the door."

"Poor you. Poor him."

"Oh, pooh! He probably won't be the last man on the lookout for easy money. The wealthy fishmonger's widow who needs a man's direction on how to spend it! Can't you just see me in a sumptuous cloak amidst the fine ladies of Tiberias?"

They both had a good laugh and spoke of other news.

An hour passed and he was on the road north to Kapharnaum again. She had become tearful at his leaving, and he remembered her farewell.

"I will be all right. Tell your mother that I am well. It's just that some days I feel all disjointed inside and lose track of things for a moment. But I'm sure that's normal in grieving. I'm going to be all right."

He would have liked to continue the conversation and learn what she meant by "feeling disjointed," but the pony was eager to pull away. He gave Miriam a wave and she returned it, and the pony moved on.

Chapter 20

THE FURNITURE ORDER IN Kapharnaum was one his father had taken. The directions were simple: find the largest house in town. That is the centurion's residence. Three doors along the street is the simpler two-storied house where the furniture is to be delivered.

The homeowners were delighted with the cartload of furniture. Their son and new wife now lived above them and had been given several of the parents' old pieces. With the help of the son, the new furniture was carried into the ground floor of the house, where a smiling wife pointed out the proper placement. The couple invited him to stay for the midday meal and a tour afterwards of the new synagogue. It had been built with dinars given by the centurion and the townspeople were proud of it.

"We are grateful for the centurion's generosity," remarked the husband. "He is a wonderful Roman! Not one of us, of course, yet he has been so helpful in many ways. Recently he even favored us with a visit for an evening meal. Imagine!"

Smiling his thanks, Yeshua declined the two-fold offer of meal and synagogue tour. He was soon on the road to Bethsaida, a short distance south of Kapharnaum on the shore of the lake.

He was elated about the coins that were wrapped in a small pouch in a hidden pocket of his cloak. It was a very good sale and his mother would be pleased. The day was sunny and warm and, with the heavy load gone, the pony trotted briskly along.

As he neared the first house of the hamlet Bethsaida, he stopped at a grassy clearing by the shore and pulled from his satchel the packet his mother had given him for his meal. The pony lowered its head and munched on his own meal of grass.

By the lake there was a ribbon of sand at the edge of water. Four boats were pulled up on the sandy beach. Men were sitting by two of the boats, mending their nets after the night's fishing. He watched them at their age-old task.

After he had eaten, Yeshua swung down from his seat and walked down to the sand and along to the first group of men, three of them. One of them was the oldest by far, sitting next to a burly man who looked to be about Yeshua's age. A younger man sat farther along at the edge of the net. Yeshua greeted them and spoke to the oldest one, saying that he had a message for Zebadya from a friend in Magdala. The man gave him a broad grin in which several teeth were missing.

"That'd be Miriam, wouldn't it?" Grunted assents came from the other two, but they did not look up from their work on the net. "What's Zeb gone and done now—put some old catch among the new?"

"No, no," smiled Yeshua. "She just wanted me to say 'hello.'"

The man squinted at him. "You haven't heavy hands from pulling the ropes of the nets. And your accent is not that of," he spat to one side, "the fine folks of Tiberias. Where you from?"

"Nearby. I am a carpenter from Nazareth."

"Well, it's a decent trade—if you're a landlubber." He pointed to the next group at the end of the line of boats. "That's Zeb and his two sons."

"Thank you."

"Huh. Good manners, too. Nazareth must be quite the civilized place."

"It's home for me."

"So be it. Trot on over there and see if Zeb will give you the time of day. Old coot."

He gave the man and his sons a wave and walked on along the narrow strand.

An older man with a weathered face and two younger men by him looked up as Yeshua approached.

"Zebadya?"

The older man eyed Yeshua .

"Now if you're here to sell us a new net, no thanks and goodbye. What we've got is plenty good enough."

Yeshua looked down at the piece of net unrolled in front of them, part of a large dragnet. It had so much mending of past torn gaps that the number of mends surpassed the original netting.

"I'm not selling nets, but it looks like you could use one."

The old man snorted. "This here net has history. Worked for twenty years and has a few more to go."

Yeshua smiled. "But with a new net there would be less mending. And fewer fish would escape through the tears."

"Hear that, boys? Ha!"

Zebadya lifted an arm to point toward a large stand of palm trees further along the curve of the shore. "See that cluster of palms?"

"Yes."

"That's Tabgha. Only a handful of houses behind those trees. Folks say you can grow anything there. Regular Garden of Eden, just like the old story. But I don't care what's on the land. Seven springs feed into the lake by Tabgha and it's the warmest water around. You with me so far?"

The two young men laughed softly but kept their eyes on their handiwork. Zebadya gave them a look. He turned his gaze back to Yeshua.

"Fish love that warm water. Warmest water in the lake, right out in front of Tabgha for, oh, how far you say, Yohannon?"

"Ten boat lengths." He raised his eyes to survey Yeshua and dropped them again as his father continued.

"That's right. At least ten lengths." He held up the part of the dragnet he had been working on. "Now, this old net here, we call it the net of good fortune. Ever since my sons were little ones, fish just can't wait to jump into this net. Spring, summer, autumn, winter. Pulls 'em in. Never fails."

"Impressive," said Yeshua.

"And good money. That's Yonah you were talking to down by the other boat. He and I have this area covered. Since my boys and his were little ones. Had some intruders come in over the years, but me and Yonah got out there a little earlier in the evening with the dragnets and the trammels and even had some casting from the shore—well, didn't leave much room. Not much room at all." He gestured toward the boats where no one was working, "We let some friends in. They pay us a little extra every catch. Me and Yonah. So that's why we don't need any new nets. Thank you anyways."

"I'm not selling nets. I came to bring you greetings from Miriam in Magdala."

"Why didn't you say that in the first place! Good woman, that Miriam. Tough on pricing a catch, but fair. Comes out all right in the end. Too bad about her husband." He motioned to a place on the sand beside him. "'Scuse me. No manners at all. Sit down here with me so's I don't get a crick in my neck looking up at you."

Yeshua squatted and sat.

"Whereabouts you from?" Zebadya asked.

"Nazareth. I'm a carpenter."

"Man of Galilea. Good." Zebadya shifted his legs. "Heard a good story from down south the other day. You might enjoy it. Shows you how some folks can get all tied up in knots." He laughed. "Or maybe it's nets."

Yeshua was silent.

"Goes like this. About a Yerushalayim fellow," Zebadya spread his arms wide. "One of the Temple folks who offer up prayers for a fee." He eyed Yeshua, who remained silent.

"I love this story," volunteered one of his sons.

"Well, now," continued the father, "he was one of the righteous folk but he must have been pretty simple minded, 'cause he was travelin' on his pony out of Yerushalayim all alone on a country road the bandits like so much. Sure enough, they got him. Stripped him. Money, clothes, the pony he was riding, everything. Beat him to a pulp and left him for dead.

"Well. He wasn't dead but he sure looked it. One of the Temple priests came along, going home to his wife and children no doubt. He was certain the fellow was a dead man; he could tell it from the other side of the road. And you know how it is, touch a dead man and you're not holy any more. So on he went. Personally, I think the bandits should have got him, but never you mind.

"Next came one of the Temple singers, a Levite. Same story. Pass on by. How he could be on a lonely road and not catch it from the bandits, I don't know, but this is s'posed to be a true story and that's the way it is sometimes.

"Now for the good part. Another fellow comes along on his horse. He sees the poor fellow and goes over to him. Smart enough to tell he is still alive and wraps him and his bruises and wounds up as best he can and puts him on his horse. Doesn't know him from Adam, but that's what he does.

"Gets him into the next town to an inn and makes sure he has water and food. Stays with him through the night, the fellow groaning and keeping him awake and all that. Next day he tells the innkeeper he has to go on, and he gives him a fistful of dinars to take care of the man and says if more is needed he'll stop by on his next trip and pay the bill. The end."

He slid a glance sideways at Yeshua. "What do you make of that, man of Nazareth?"

Yeshua considered the question. He spoke slowly when at last he answered. "The man who helped was a Samaritan."

Zebadya's eyes opened wide. "You betcha. Very good. Boys, this fellow has a head on his shoulders!"

Yeshua continued. "The story is a good one and reminds those who hear it—you, me, your sons, and others—that the ways of the Lord are not confined to a particular family or group.

"So you think the Samaritan—word is, they are the heathen—the Samaritan did the right thing?"

"Yes. But I would not call the helpful man a heathen."

"Me, neither," said Zebadya. "May the Lord have mercy on the Samaritans and wither the snooty religious types who don't have the heart to help somebody who's down and out."

The circle considered this statement.

"Back to what we were talking about before. You and Miriam. Friends?"

"My parents are. My mother. My father died recently."

"Sorry to hear about that," said Zebadya. "Same with Miriam. Hosea was a good man, one of the best, but he was too easy on us fisher folk. Couldn't cut as sharp a deal as his wife."

"That's what I've heard."

Zebadya nodded. "Fisher folks, we been out on the water most of the night. Like to have some haggling to tune us up in the mornin'.

"Well, now. Introduce you to my sons." His head nodded towards them. "One with the scraggly beard is the youngster, Yohannon. One with a nice full beard is his older brother Yaakob." They nodded to Yeshua.

"Now, getting back to Hosea's widow. How she seem to you?"

"We talked for a while this morning. She seemed fine. But then when I was leaving, she said something about a strange feeling that comes over her now and then."

Zebadya smacked the sand with one hand. "Hear that, boys! Just what I was talking about."

"You've noticed something?"

"A little bit after Hosea passed, she started getting kind of moody. Not as sharp on the pricing as before. Doesn't have a heart for bargaining sometimes."

Yohannon spoke up. "For the Lord's sake, father, she's lost her husband!"

"True, true. But it didn't feel like grieving somehow. And in recent days, she stops talking in the middle of a conversation and stands there like she's listening to something inside her. Strangest thing. Not like the Miriam of old."

"Maybe she got witchy when that wild man came through," said Yaakob.

Yeshua's ears pricked up. "Wild man?"

"Now, now, bit of a stretch there," cautioned Zebadya.

"Black hair and beard? Shorter than me?"

Yaakob and Yohannon both nodded, their full attention now on Yeshua.

"Same name as mine," noted Yohannon.

"My kinsman," replied Yeshua.

"Really?" Yohannon was eager to hear more.

"Now, boys, don't go getting all excited," their father said and turned to their visitor. "He stayed two days and got all the boys whooped up about bringing the people back to the straight and narrow of the Lord. Talked about purification by water further down by the river, that kind of thing. Y'ask me, we got enough water. He could do it right here."

"Father, it's closer to Yerushalayim than hereabouts," protested Yaakob.

"Maybe so, but we got need for purification around here." He gave Yeshua a sideways glance. "Y'hear about how Antipas married his brother's wife?"

"Yes. Word does get around."

"No matter to me as long as he doesn't levy another tax on fish. Needs the money, though, for all his fancy buildings and parties." Zebadya snorted. "Me, I just want to fish."

"Yonah's second son went," said Yohannon. "Philippos."

"Yes. But then that boy always has been interested in the wider world. And he takes his religion seriously." Zebadya turned again to Yeshua. "Philippos. Greek name. Like his younger brother—Andreas. But the first one, Yonah got his say on naming. Insisted on a regular local name, Shimeon."

Zebadya peered down the beach. "Shimeon's the big fellow. Sometimes he and my boys have a partnership. Nights I want to stay in with the wife, if you catch my meaning.

"The family fuss came about because Yonah married a woman of Greek descent. Goes way back. But she goes right along to the synagogue in Kapharnaum like the rest of us." He peered out at the lake. "Unless the fish are running heavy."

"I wanted to go with the wild man," said Yohannon, and his brother nodded. "Me, too."

Zebadya snorted. "Maybe you did. But nobody's going to snatch you two away unless he cares more about people than ranting and railing." He looked at Yeshua. "Am I right?"

Yeshua smiled. "He asked me to go with him but I turned him down."

The older man turned back to his sons. "Y'see, boys. This fellow has more common sense than you two." He eyed Yeshua. "Your arms look good and strong. Want to stay around till tonight? You and me could take shore duty on the dragnet while the boys take out the other end in the boat and circle around with it."

"Thanks but I need to get back home."

"Give you a dozen fish for your help. And the wife will bake up some loaves of bread to take home tomorrow."

Yeshua smiled. "That's a great offer, but I really need to get going." He rose to his feet. "I'd appreciate it if you keep an eye on Miriam. If things don't seem right, please send us word. Yeshua's family, Nazareth."

Zebadya and his sons rose to their feet also. "Will do." He shook hands with Yeshua and turned to his sons. "C'mon, you shake his hand, too. Not often a man of good sense and caring for others comes along." They shook hands with Yeshua and the old man smiled. "Even if he's not a fisherman."

Chapter 21

STORM CLOUDS PILED OVER the northern mountains in late afternoon, moving south. Under darkening skies, Yeshua made it home just before the heavy rain began.

At supper, Miriam was distracted by concern for Yehudah and the shepherds. She barely touched her food, and gazed at the ceiling as if warding off the thunder and lightning.

"Mother," said Yaakob. She continued to gaze upwards.

"Mother," he repeated. She dropped her eyes from the ceiling to meet Yaakob's even look, his chin resting on one hand. "They surely have reached the spring grazing field by now," he said, "and the hut is there. It will give them protection from the storm."

"I know," she said. "I was remembering a night long ago when shepherds came." She looked at Yeshua. "In Bethlehem."

Suddenly the outer door burst open and Yehudah and three other boys, barely young men, dripped their way to the dining room.

"Yehudah!" Miriam rose from the table. She turned. "Elisheva, Rebekah. Quickly, the drying cloths." The girls rose and went.

Yehudah spoke. "Mother, my brothers, there was not room for us all in the hut. So I brought them here. I have the honor of presenting Oren, Yishaq, and Semuel, excellent shepherds. Yaso is guarding the sheep pen from the hut."

The older brothers at the table stared. Miriam strode to the door and closed it firmly. "We are glad for your presence among us," she said as the young men turned towards her. They bowed. "Will Yaso be all right?" she asked.

"We drew straws. He wanted to stay anyway. I told him he is now general of the sheep. And we gave him all our food."

"Well, there's enough here for the four of you," Miriam exclaimed. "But first let's get you dried off."

Elisheva and Rebekah returned with armfuls of towels and distributed them to the foursome. As Yehudah rubbed his head dry, he exclaimed, "We have had an adventure!"

"Yes, yes," said his mother, "we must hear all about it. Elisheva, take them in by the hearth fire to warm them. I hear teeth chattering. Rebekah, bring the old cloaks we washed the other day, so that they may have warm clothes!" Elisheva went, with the youths in tow.

"My, my." said Yosa as Miriam returned to the table with more earthenware plates. "Our brother appears to be much older than when we saw him last."

"Indeed," nodded Yaakob, a smile twitching at his lips.

"Yes," mused Yeshua. "I can hardly wait to hear his tale."

In a short while they did, as the shepherds and Yehudah crowded in with the others at the dining table.

Yosa broke the silence. "And what was your adventure?"

Yehudah swallowed a mouthful of bread and answered. "A lost ewe lamb."

He and Oren reached for more bread but Yaakob waved their hands away from the bowl.

"No more," he warned. "Not until we hear your tale."

Yehudah leaned back. "It was just before sunset. We could tell a storm was coming and we were herding the flock up the hillside to the safety of the sheepfold." His hands made a large circle in the air. "The clouds were curling and turning darker and lightning flashed to the north of us. I was at the rear of the flock with Semuel. We urged the sheep on, and it was a relief when all were in and Oren closed the gate."

He paused and reached for more bread. Yaakob pulled it away. "Continue," he said.

"But Yaso stood by the gate doing the count, and he called out, 'one missing!' And Yaso knows his numbers so it was true."

Yehudah looked hungrily toward the bread bowl. "Oh, all right," Yaakob said as he pushed the bowl back. The hands of the four youths took all of the remaining bread.

"I looked back down the hill," continued Yehudah. "No sheep struggling upward to us. Semuel nudged me and pointed off to the side to a ravine at the base of the hill."

Semuel smiled and nodded.

"It was far from the path we had taken up the hill. The rain began, only drops at first, then more steadily. I thought, 'Only one sheep that can be found tomorrow.' And I turned to run to the hut."

He pointed a finger at Semuel, who was basking in the attention.

"Semuel was running the other way—down the hill. What could I do but follow him? We reached the bottom and walked toward the ravine. As we drew closer, the wind was rising and the thickets snatched at our cloaks. But we pushed on."

Yehudah paused. All eyes were on him.

Yaakob sighed. "Little brother, enough drama."

"And there," Yehudah twirled his wrist, "there before us, caught in a thicket, was a ewe lamb, all frightened and bleating her heart out!"

Miriam rose. "I say, good for Yehudah and especially for Semuel, a good shepherd of his flock!" Applause erupted around the table as Semuel's eyes glowed and a broad smile broke out on Yehudah's face.

Applauding with the others, Yeshua turned to Yaakob. "Little brother is not so belittling of shepherds tonight."

Yaakob smiled, "So it seems. He has learned a good lesson."

CHAPTER 22

THE NEXT MORNING WAS a beautiful Galilean day, with a clear blue sky and the air washed clean by the storm. The three young shepherds and Yehudah were off at the third cockcrow, eager to reunite with Yaso, general of the sheep. They carried with them a bountiful basket of food from Miriam and a joyful account of their reception the evening before.

After the morning meal, Yeshua remained at the table. The others had dispersed—his sisters to their household chores and his brothers to the workshop. There was an unspoken agreement among all that his successful trip to Capernaum merited a day of rest.

He watched Miriam clear the dishes. "You have never told me more of the story," he complained to her back. "I want to know more. Now is the time."

She turned. Her eyes told him that she knew exactly what he was asking.

"Very well." Miriam looked about, but no one was within hearing range. She walked to the table and sat in her usual chair. She took a small leather pouch from her apron pocket and reached again to bring up the coins Yeshua had brought home. She began counting them.

"Perhaps that centurion in Kapharnaum will buy furniture from us," she said.

"Mother, this is not about furniture."

"I know." She leaned back in her chair and gave him a steady look. "So much has happened since I was a girl.

A long time ago. I convinced myself that it was a fanciful dream, that man in the white robe."

"Now is the time. I want to know the rest," said Yeshua firmly.

Miriam leaned forward. "I have been thinking the same thing. Your father's final wish was the turning point. There were inklings all along. And lately, the dream you had."

She sat back in her chair. "When you were a small child you were like other children, playful and inquisitive and joyful all the time at the wonders of the world. But in your third year you began talking—really talking. The things young children talk about, but more. You spoke of places you had been, but we had been with you all the time and you had not been there. And you described several places that we knew about but had never been. I was struck by it and thought it simply idle chatter of half-formed dreams from conversation that you had overheard. As it continued, I thought, how can this be?

"Then a time came when such talk stopped. You were simply a bright young child who had good days and bad days.

"You grew. You learned—oh, how you learned! Your mind was like a sponge, absorbing everything around you." She smiled at the memory. "You had insights that were beyond your youth. My friends—other young mothers— were jealous at first. Then it became a joke among us. They would say, 'Watch that Yeshua, Miriam, he's bound to be a famous rabbi and Nazareth won't be big enough for him!'" Her smile faded.

"But then came that Passover in Yerushalayim when you were twelve."

A pause as they looked at each other.

"At first I was frightened when you said that you were in your father's house. But then—it made sense. And now . . . Yeshua, what did you do to Shimeon?"

"Shimeon? Nothing."

"This cannot be true. He was healed and the fever broken."

"As you said, a wonderful thing."

"It was a sign. What did you do? Tell me."

"The same as we all did. I kept wetting the cloth and dampening him all over his body to calm the fever."

"What else?" Her voice was insistent as she leaned toward him. "You must have done something else."

"Nothing, mother. I just sat there with him, taking my turn."

"No more than that?"

"No more than that."

She sat back in her chair. "I'm sorry. I was mistaken."

"I did say a prayer."

"A prayer?"

"One that I had heard father say many times. When I was of an age to accompany him to the sick and the dying."

"Ah. And what were the words?"

He told her. She pursed her lips. "And truly, that was all?"

"Yes."

"I went with him at times," she mused. "That is what he would say. But none of them were healed."

She poured the coins onto the table and began to count them.

"It was the price we had agreed upon," Yeshua reminded her. "The coins are all there."

She stopped and looked at him with angry eyes. "I don't care about the coins. I was hoping. . . ." Her voice trailed off.

"Hoping for what?"

"That it would not come to this. That you were only a bright boy and you would grow up and marry like other men and have children of your own. A simple, easy story."

She looked hard at him and her words spilled out. "But it has never been easy. Lately it has all come back to me. The awful time with my parents and Yosef's parents and after you were born the shame of a quick marriage in Bethlehem with the words of the ceremony by a rabbi we hoped we would never see again. And then the terrible dream of your father's that I could not understand. Suddenly it was all scramble, scramble, we must go. To Egypt. *Now.*" She sighed.

"What have you been hoping for?"

"A lovely wedding feast would have been nice."

"No, now. What are you hoping for?"

She reached out a hand and caressed his face as she had on the night Yosef died.

"I want you to stay with me and care for me when I am old."

"I will," Yeshua protested. "Don't say foolish things."

Miriam sighed again. "My son, the time is near when you must fulfill the purpose of the Lord."

Yeshua looked deeply into her eyes and saw all the mothering and nurturing and caring through the years. Of him, her firstborn. And now, fear.

"What are you afraid of?" he asked.

"I don't want to lose you. But something is happening. Things are coming together. Your kinsman's visit. Your brother Shimeon. Your dream, so much like your father's dreams even though he was not your father in the sense of the world. Something in you is awakening. It soon will be time for you to go."

He was silent.

"You are my son." Her eyes remained fixed on his as she pushed the leather pouch and the coins aside and leaned forward on the table. "I nursed you as a baby. I held you close as a child when you fell and skinned your knees. I have watched you grow into a kind, compassionate man. And now I must give you up to the Lord."

He kept his silence, his eyes on hers.

"Sometimes," she cried out, "oh, Yeshua, may the Lord forgive me, sometimes I wish I were back in that garden with Gabriel all those years ago and I would say 'no!' No, not me! Thank you very much but please go choose some one else. I want a normal life. A life without the haunting presence of what I was told about a new beginning."

She dropped her eyes from his and pushed at the coins.

"I will tell you now what else Gabriel said to me long ago. His words are etched on my heart. I have made my peace with them in these past weeks. As you now must make your own peace."

She held her hand to her mouth for a moment, re-membering. When she spoke again, the words were clear and distinct.

"He said, the child born of you comes for all people. He will show the way of the Lord.

"He said, your son will bring a message with these words, 'The time is fulfilled, and the kingdom of the Lord is among you; turn to the Lord and believe in this good news.'

"He said, one day he will stand in the synagogue here in Nazareth. The scroll will be open at the words of Isaiah, and Yeshua will read, 'The Spirit of the Lord is upon me, be-cause he has anointed me to bring good news to the desti-tute. He has sent me to proclaim release to the captives and recovery of sight to the blind, to let the oppressed go free, to proclaim the year of the Lord's favor now and forever.' And then he will say, 'Today this scripture has been fulfilled in your hearing.'"

Miriam fell silent. Yeshua was reflecting on her startling words when she lifted her eyes to him.

"My beloved son, the message is clear. I have hoped and wished otherwise all these years. It is why I have said nothing to you until now.

"Yeshua, you are the One who is to come. It is a new beginning, as Gabriel said. You are the Messiah. It is the only explanation."

The words hung in the air between them. Yeshua stared at her. Her eyes were steady, with no tears.

At last he pushed back from the table. His chair fell backwards as he stood.

"Mother, enough! I cannot take it all in. I must go for a walk to calm myself."

He managed to make his way to the door. His last sight of Miriam was of her steady gaze following him to the door.

He struggled through the town. Past the well, his ears deaf to the gossip of the women. Past all the houses which he knew so well. He could recite the names of every occupant. Past the greetings of townspeople. He did not respond. To the edge of the town where the village gave way to the fields.

At last he could walk no further and he leaned against an olive tree. He felt faint and slid to the ground.

"O Lord, heavenly father, show me what your will is for me," he prayed aloud. There was no answer. His eyes closed, and he dozed, exhausted by the day.

The sun set and night came on. He was awakened by his mother's touch on his arm. "Yeshua, come home." He climbed to his feet and went with her.

Chapter 23

THAT NIGHT HE DREAMED of the river.

He dreamed he was in a long line of men two abreast. Some were praying quietly as the line slowly moved forward to the bank of the river. The day was warm. A light breeze swirled the desert sand over by the grove of trees where the tents were pitched. He could see women walking among the trees, waiting for their turn to form a line. A child's sudden cry came, followed by the soft voice of a mother. The cry subsided.

Nearing the river an older man stood by the path. "Single file, now. Single file," he chanted. The line thinned and reformed.

To his right there was another line of men, coming from the river. Their line was uneven. Their cloaks were drenched. Most held up their hands in prayer. Others softly sang a Psalm of the Temple. The faces of all shone with radiant joy.

He continued to move forward. At last the man ahead of him reached the river. A boy in shepherd's clothes was clambering up the side of the bank, rough clothing drenched, his face glowing. The river was not deep and barely ten arm lengths wide at this part of its course southward.

A young man wearing a much-mended white cloak held up a hand for the line to wait. In the narrow river ahead, a man was raised from the river water by two of the three persons there. The young man in the white cloak nodded and the man in front of Yeshua carefully stepped on stones that formed a path down to the river and waded toward the three men. One of them was his kinsman.

Another nod and his turn came. He felt a great exultation within himself as he slowly waded to the middle of the river. His kinsman Yohannon turned to him and his eyes widened.

"You!" he said. One of the other men moved near to help Yeshua fall backwards into the water but Yohannon waved him away. "I will help this one," he said. He moved to Yeshua's side and placed one arm around his back.

"Do you pledge your life to the way of the Lord and to fear no man in this world," his kinsman murmured in his ear.

"Yes, with all my heart."

Yohannon placed his other hand on Yeshua's chest and he went down into the cold water.

Yeshua awoke with a start, damp with sweat. He was in the room he shared with Yaakob. He heard the cock crow. It was almost dawn.

He rose quietly so as not to awaken the others and pulled on his workday clothing. On soft steps he made his way through the house and went to a bench in the garden.

There he prayed and meditated until the sun cleared the treetops and his mother called him to breakfast.

Chapter 24

Yeshua was silent and withdrawn at the morning table. Miriam and the others glanced at him from time to time as Shimeon prattled on about the wheel he was helping Yaakob to make in the workshop. Yeshua took no notice.

After the simple meal of melon, bread and cheese, he left the house and retraced his steps of the day before.

The synagogue groundskeeper was sweeping the steps and gave him a friendly nod. As he passed a corner he saw a band of boys chattering away as they walked to their morning class at the synagogue.

Nazareth had grown since he was a child. The space between the older stone houses had filled with newer houses as newcomers came who wished to be close to the place of worship.

He paused at the street corner across from the town's well. A large group surrounded it, mostly younger women. One of the women looked over at him and curtsied, prompting an outburst of giggles from the others around her. He smiled and walked on.

At last he reached the tree he had slept against the night before and sat down against it. The olives were almost ripe, he noticed.

He sat there until the sun was near midday and then he rose and walked home.

HE SPOKE BRIEFLY WITH his mother as the others were gathering from the separate parts of the house for the midday meal. She nodded and turned to help Rebekah and Elisheva bring the food to the table for the main meal of the day.

Yeshua's usual seat was at the right hand of Miriam. Today he stood behind it and turned to Yaakob. "Brother," he said quietly, "move to this seat. I will sit next to Shimeon."

Yaakob began to protest and Yeshua gave him a nudge as he moved behind him to the far end of the table, next to the youngest. Shimeon was delighted and began a cheery conversation about progress in the workroom. Miriam silenced him as they all sat. She looked down the table at Yeshua. He nodded.

She turned to her right and cleared her throat. "Yaakob, please say the blessing."

Yaakob gave Yeshua a startled look. Yeshua, wondered the others, always gave the blessing. Always. Yaakob turned to his mother. She nodded.

It was a very quiet meal.

When they had finished, the two sisters rose to clear the table. Yeshua motioned them back to their seats. "I have something to say to all of you," he declared in a firm tone.

They stared. All but Miriam. There was a look in her eyes that Yeshua had never seen before, a look of calm resignation.

"I am going away today," Yeshua said, "to see our kinsman at the river. I do not know how long it will be before I return. Therefore I am passing headship of the house to Yaakob."

"But why is this?" protested Yaakob. He continued in a sarcastic tone, "I had not expected that the crazy man would act so as to make me head of the household!"

"It is not his decision. It is mine," Yeshua calmly replied.

"My brother, have you spoken with our mother about this sudden dereliction of responsibility?"

"Yes, I have."

At the other end of the table, Miriam nodded and placed a hand on Yaakob's arm. He shook it off.

"Why such an abrupt leavetaking? Why did you not talk of it, hint of it, give us some advance warning of this incredible action! By the Lord, we are your family!"

Nods of agreement around the table. Except for Shimeon.

"Can I come with you?" he asked excitedly. Yeshua smiled at him. "No. You are needed here."

Bewildered, Yosa asked, "Who will bring us customers?"

"You will."

"But I know little about such matters. I am a carpenter."

"You have seen the excellent work that Yaakob does. Because you know it well, you will be able to speak to others and to show samples of Yaakob's workmanship."

"Am I to be an old maid?" cried Elisheva. "Who will arrange a marriage for me?"

"Yaakob will. He and I have spoken of late about prospects in Nazareth for a suitable husband. He will guide you." Yeshua glanced at Rebekah. "Do not worry, little sister. You will do well also."

There were further questions and he answered them all, including the final one from Yaakob about whether Yeshua was now to be the next crazy man. "No," he replied.

He remained seated at the table with his mother after the others had left. Miriam rose and went to the hearth in the other room. She was out of sight but he could hear the *chink* as she moved the loose stone, behind which she hid the household moneybox.

She returned to the table holding the box and one of her leather pouches.

"It is all very well for you to go off. I am here, and I am still your mother. As you know, mothers worry about their children, even when they grow to your age."

She raised the lid of the box and swiftly counted out coins. "Just so I won't be worrying about you lying impoverished in a ditch by the side of some unknown road, here are thirty pieces of silver." She placed them in the pouch and tied the cord at the top. "If you need work, I'm sure you'll find it. Send messages as often as you can."

"Mother," he said, "that money is for you."

Miriam shook her head and rose again from the table, carrying the pouch. She walked around the table to where he sat. She put the pouch down in front of him and stood behind, her arms around his chest. She rested her head on the top of his.

"You said you are leaving today."

"Yes. My knapsack is ready."

"Well, then. I will walk you to the door."

He stood and picked up the pouch.

They walked slowly to the wooden door. Yeshua reached to the row of hooks by it and pulled down a knapsack and his cloak. He opened the door. They both stepped through it and stood.

"Tell me," Miriam said in a husky voice, "that we—that I—will see you again."

"Yes." He smiled. "It seems I will read a passage from Isaiah in the synagogue here."

"I am glad you are my son," she said. "May the Lord be with you."

"I am very, very glad that you are my mother," he told her. "I love you. May the Lord be also with you."

She stifled a sob and leaned up on tiptoe to kiss him on his cheek.

"Thank you," she said. "Thank you." She turned and went back into the house, closing the door gently behind her.

Chapter 26

FROM THE RIVERBANK THE Baptizer concluded his daily call to a renewal of commitment to the Lord with his prophecy.

"Now, now is the Day of the Lord!" Yohannon shouted. "The Messiah is coming! Prepare the way! Today repent of all your sins and waywardness and failings—come now to the river to be purified and you will have a new birth in the Lord!" He turned and waded into the river.

The crowd of men who had been listening shifted and formed a line. Two abreast, shoulder to shoulder, they shuffled forward to the riverbank. Each man's heart was filled with anticipation of the ritual to come and longing for the promised liberation to a new life.

The day had begun sunny but now the clouds overhead were darkening. A light breeze swirled the desert sand over by the grove of trees where the tents were pitched. Yeshua could see women walking among the trees, waiting for their turn to form a line. A child's sudden cry came, followed by the soft voice of a mother. The cry subsided.

Nearing the river an older man stood by the path. "Single file, now. Single file," he chanted as he eyed the clouds overhead. The line thinned and reformed. There was another line of men, coming from the river. Their line was irregular and uneven but they moved briskly along. Their cloaks were drenched. Most held up their hands in prayer. Others softly sang a praise psalm of the Temple. The faces of all shone with radiant joy.

Yeshua continued to move slowly forward. At last the man ahead of him reached the river. A boy in shepherd's clothes was clambering up the side of the bank. From his shaggy hair rivulets of water dripped, further wetting his soaked rough clothing. He was smiling broadly at the men in the line moving forward. "What a glorious day," he shouted. "Praise the Lord!"

A young man wearing a much-mended white cloak held up a hand for the line to wait. In the river a man was raised from the water by two assistants of the third person there. The young man in the white cloak nodded and the person in front of Yeshua carefully stepped on stones that formed a path down to the river and waded toward the three men. The third man was Yeshua's kinsman.

Another nod and his turn came. He felt a great peace within himself as he waded to the middle of the river. Yohannon turned to him and his eyes widened.

"You!" he said. One of the assistants moved near to help Yeshua with the immersion but Yohannon waved him away. "Philippos, I will help this one," he said. He moved to Yeshua's side and placed an arm around his back.

"Do you wish to be reborn from above to a new life in the Lord?"

"Yes." Yeshua answered.

"Do you pledge your life to the way of the Lord and to fear no man in this world?"

"Yes, with all my heart."

Yohannon placed his other hand on Yeshua's chest and he went down into the cold river water. Deep, deep down in the water he descended and he felt a huge weight, as of all human history, gathering and pressing him down. And then he was rising to freedom, rising to gasp a fresh breath of air.

A sudden thunderclap split the sky and the wind began to pick up. On the bank, the young man in the white cloak shouted above the wind, "No more today. No more today. Take shelter."

Yohannon's arms encircled Yeshua's waist. "Stay with me."

"No. I must go into the desert to learn what is set before me."

"You will find it here. Look around at all the people. They are hungry for the truth of the Lord. The time has come. Stay."

The steady gaze of Yeshua silenced him and Yohannon dropped his hands.

"The time has come indeed," Yeshua said. "Your prophecy is now complete." He turned away.

As he climbed up the riverbank his heart was calm and he moved with a sureness of purpose. He looked up. Overhead a dove was circling. The first drops of rain fell. Yeshua laughed a great, joyful laugh and strode toward the desert.

A cave was waiting for him. A cave with a pool of water in front of it and a small carob tree growing alongside.